A MARRIAGE FOR SHOW

TALL, DARK AND DRIVEǸ BOOK 5

BARBARA DELEO

A MARRIAGE FOR SHOW

TALL, DARK AND DRIVEN - BOOK 5

Christo's story

by Barbara DeLeo

This story was originally published, in part, as *Contract for Marriage*

FANCY A FREE NOVELLA?

Waiting on Forever—*Alex's story—is the prequel to my Tall, Dark and Driven series and is available* **exclusively** *and* **free** *for subscribers to my reader list.*

You can claim your free novella at the end of this book!

1

A kaleidoscope of color sparkled overhead as Ruby Fleming kicked toward the surface of her late parents' Olympic-sized swimming pool. The cool water across her skin was a relief from the sticky summer heat of a Brentwood Bay evening and the heart-wrenching turmoil of the last few weeks. It seemed too cruel to be real that the precious life inside her had lost both a father and grandmother in the space of a month.

Ruby broke through the surface, tossed her long hair over her shoulder, and flicked water from her eyes. When she'd got her breath back and focused, her heart constricted in her chest as she froze. An imposing figure stood shadowed by the wisteria-covered terrace above the pool, a selection of designer luggage at his feet.

Dread crawled the length of her spine. The last of the mourners had left in the days after her mom's funeral, and Stella the housekeeper hadn't been here when Ruby had arrived in such a hurry from New York. She *should* be the only person on the estate.

This six-foot plus package of sizzling masculinity made a lie of that.

Her heart beat harder as she waded in shoulder-deep water to the pool's tiled edge. How long had he been standing there, watching her, waiting?

Razor-edged suit. Vanilla crème shirt against mocha skin. A stance of unleashed determination. Her stomach somersaulted as she blinked and then frowned. There was something familiar...

The man stepped forward, the classic angles of his face grim, and the sense of familiarity burned deeper.

"My condolences for the loss of your mother. She was a very generous and caring woman. She'll be missed."

The words, like tumbling river stones, washed over her in a wave of realization. His voice was more mature than she remembered, but its sensuality, the way it sang in her ears and rocketed straight to her core, was the same as ten years ago.

"Christo."

She swallowed away his name as her pulse sprinted. The month-long scar of tears and regret she wore like a brand bit deep. "I'm sorry you couldn't get here sooner. The funeral was Friday."

As he moved closer, the dark cloud stamped across his face shifted a fraction, and on reflex, Ruby splayed the fingers of both hands across her bare belly beneath the water—holding herself together, keeping every part of her private.

She hadn't seen Christo Mantazis in a decade, but knew being around him caused her to lose focus on what was right, what was important. And nothing was more important than this baby.

He'd been nineteen then, when he'd moved out of the

quarters he shared with his mother, Stella, the estate's housekeeper. No longer having an impressive street address or influential people to mix with, he'd tried to stay connected with Ruby's privileged world by telling her he was in love with her. Only when her father caught them and confronted him did Christo back away. Fast. He'd also been seen with other women at the polo club and the yacht club, trying to make connections that would stick.

She'd asked Christo one question on the day her father had banished him from the estate and her life—did he want her, or the package she came with? He'd left the house without giving her an answer. Without fighting for their relationship. Without fighting for *her*. And he'd taken a precious part of her heart with him.

"I've come from the airport." His voice lowered and took on a harder edge. "We were in Greece when we heard."

We. Did he mean himself and his mother? Or a girlfriend. A wife.

Ruby craned her neck, searching, and kept her voice steady when she asked, "Is Stella with you?"

"Mom is back at my apartment. She's upset about Antonia's death, especially distraught that the funeral was held so quickly. I've brought my aunt from Greece to stay with her until matters are finalized."

Ruby dipped her shoulders lower, glad for the cool water on her overheated skin. Seeing Christo again unsettled her more than she'd ever imagined, particularly when he was talking in riddles.

"Which *matters*?"

He dragged gold-rimmed aviator glasses from his face, and her breath hitched as his onyx gaze pinned hers. Glossy black hair licked the burnished skin of his face and framed a masculine jaw darkened by the shadow of travel-induced stubble. His lips, lips she'd once hungered for, were set in a rigid line. Ten years might've passed, but he was as striking...no, *more* striking than she remembered.

He tapped the sunglasses against a thigh standing taut under the fine suit fabric. Memories of being tangled in his arms rippled through her, and her stomach looped.

He reached for his jacket's inside pocket and withdrew a white envelope.

"This contains a bank check for an amount to cover my purchase of your share of this property." His voice cut through her, face impassive. "In a perfect world, I wouldn't intrude on your grief so soon, but I've no choice. My offer's more than generous."

Ruby blinked. Her *share* of this property? She was an only child. Her mom didn't have anyone else to leave the house to. She touched her palm to her belly—well, no one her mother had known about.

Trying to clear her mind, she shook her hair and water droplets rained on the surface of the pool. "What offer?"

He bent and scooped up the large red towel at his feet and held it open invitingly. "Come out of the water and we'll discuss it." The power of his look and the cold, detached tone didn't match the broad expanse of his open arms.

Ruby's blood chilled and she clutched her body tighter. "I'm fine where I am, thank you." She wasn't moving from the privacy of the water. He didn't need to see more of her ripening body than he already had. "Tell me, Christo, what offer?"

He stood silent for a moment, then tossed the towel and envelope on the ornate iron table. He pulled up a chair before effortlessly folding his six-plus frame into it. Drumming his fingers on the tabletop, he lifted his chin and fixed her with a firm stare.

"You return to New York when?"

The early evening breeze shuffled leaves at the corner of the tennis court, and despite the heat of the day, Ruby shivered. He'd avoided her question and his tone was rough, careless—so different from the secret, sensual way he'd spoken to her in the past. She looked down and swallowed past the lump in her throat. Her world had been turned on its head in the last month, nothing was clear anymore.

In a matter of weeks she'd learned of her pregnancy and that the father—a man she'd dated on and off—had died in a car wreck. Now her mother, who she hadn't seen in years, was gone and it was as if she were being pulled into some frightening black hole. And here was Christo, a shock in itself, using phrases like "share of this property".

Christo had changed. The fiercely passionate boy was now an intense man who radiated heat and raw energy, and something wild and pulsing strained beneath his surface.

He'd asked when she was returning to New York. She lifted her chin.

It was none of his business.

"I'm not making any big decisions right now."

"You wouldn't come back here to live." The bold certainty in his statement stung. "You haven't been back since you were a child."

A child? She gripped the frigid edge of the pool. He'd thought of her as a child back then? She'd been a young adult, and there had been nothing childlike in the way she'd felt about him. And nothing innocent in the inexcusable way he'd treated her. Leaving without an explanation. Never contacting her again.

Eighteen and ecstatically happy in his arms, it had devastated her when her father had confronted him with the truth of his womanizing and banished Christo from the house. When she'd angrily gone after him to explain how much he'd hurt her, Christo had turned the anger back on her, asking why she hadn't stood up for him. Couldn't he see that he'd broken the trust she'd so carefully placed in him? Taken her from the heights of sizzling passion to the depths of confusion? If her father's allegations weren't true, then Christo would've stayed and fought for her. Not walked out of her life. Of that, she was certain.

The double hurt that had bored through her all those years ago leaked into her words. "I've been back." She scanned his inscrutable face. *When you were on your annual trip to Greece.* In truth, returning to Brentwood Bay on those few occasions had been difficult, hurtful. Leaving her home town because she couldn't live with the secret of her mother's long-term affair—and the broken family it had caused—had seemed her only option then, but in recent years she'd yearned for a sense of her old self, her heritage.

Being away for most of a decade had meant she'd managed to avoid Christo. Whenever his name was mentioned when she was back, she'd tried to blank out the details. He hadn't been here since her father had told him all those years ago to never come back, and he had no business being here now.

She asked again. "What *offer*, Christo?"

Dark shadows passed across his chiseled features, and he leaned back in the chair, scrutinizing her. "Antonia didn't discuss her will? She told you *nothing* of her plans?"

Her heart drummed in her chest. Surely he knew that she and her mother hadn't been close. "No, she didn't. Her death was so sudden—her heart problem had been undetected. Her lawyer has asked to see me tomorrow to discuss her wishes. I'm sure everything will be in order." A stab deep in her throat reminded her how little she'd known of her mother in the last few years. Forgiveness for the pain her mother had caused their family with her affair hadn't come easily to Ruby. Now she'd never have the chance to tell her mother she'd loved her despite the past. She blinked that tragedy away.

She scanned Christo's face, the dark lashes that framed his unforgiving stare, and she swallowed. Why was he mentioning estates and offers when it was *her* mother who'd been buried this week? "Tell me what you know, Christo."

"You and I are joint beneficiaries of the major part of your mother's estate. This property." His jaw set firmer. "I'm here to buy you out."

For a moment, the water around her seemed to move before she realized it was her body that was swaying. She grabbed hold of the tiled edge to steady herself, his words pulsing in her head. They didn't make sense. None of this did. "You can't... she wouldn't..."

In a second he was on his feet, his sleeve pushed up, holding out a strong hand to her.

"Ruby, take my hand." She stared at his broad, welcoming palm and tried to straighten everything in her mind, wanting someone to save her from this nightmare.

Anyone but him.

He was to have a half share of this house? Her childhood home? The place that should pass to her child as it had to five generations of Flemings before?

No.

His voice deepened, commanded, "Ruby, get out of the pool."

Mindless, she put her hand in his and the second their skin connected, a bolt of heat flared through her, a connection so strong it stole the breath from her lungs. With frightening speed, he lifted her out until she stood dripping on his beautifully polished shoes. As her cool hand warmed in his sure grip, she slowly looked up into his face and her throat closed.

Eyes the color of midnight sent a smoldering rope throughout her body, and she dragged in a bigger breath as he surveyed her from top to toe. This wasn't happening. Couldn't be. He reached for the towel and placed it around her shoulders.

Grabbing the loose corners, she rushed to conceal the curve of her belly. "I don't believe you." Her voice was rough and raw. "My mother would never leave half the house to you after what you did. We might've had our difficulties, but she'd never want to hurt me."

Holding her steady, the strength in his hands burned through the towel, his polished, perfect male scent invading her senses. "The documentation is succinct and clear. You'll receive all the details from your mother's lawyer in time, but we'll resolve ownership now to keep things simple."

Ruby sank into the iron chair behind her, limbs loose, skin chilling. "Why would she do this? We hadn't spoken much lately, but I'd have thought that with something so significant..."

He took the chair opposite and leaned back, twilight causing the bronze of his skin to deepen and shadows to settle in the contours of his face. "So I could buy your share."

"You spoke to her about it in person?"

For the briefest moment, a soft change swept across his face before it vanished. "She was a complex but deeply caring woman. We spoke many times. She knew you had no interest in returning here to stay, so she wanted to offer you an easy exit. At the same time, she'd ensure the house went to someone who appreciated it."

With frozen fingers, Ruby pulled the towel tight across her body as his stare hardened once more. Her father had banished him, and Christo had been furious at her father's decree. The son of an immigrant housekeeper, he'd seen her as an open door into another, more privileged world. What on earth had persuaded her mother to leave this property to Christo Mantazis now? He'd obviously convinced her that either he'd made a mistake all those years ago or, by some miracle, he'd changed.

From the way he sat, inscrutable and closed, but with his gaze skimming her body, Ruby believed neither. She raised her chin a fraction. "I can't think why she'd have wanted to provide for you, but why didn't she just give you money? Why a share of our house?"

With an ironic smile, he flicked his wrist and a designer watch jangled against the table. "It's not money I need, Ruby." His voice was smooth and self-assured.

The exquisite suit, the brand name luggage—he'd come a very long way in ten years. "Then, what?"

He leaned forward, a forearm resting on the table edge, and the crisp, clean scent of him surrounded her. "My mother has lived in this house for decades. It's the only home she's ever known in this country and the only place she'll be happy. You haven't lived here for years."

Her mind raced. Although she felt for Stella—losing a close friend and her job at the same time—Ruby couldn't possibly sell this house, her baby's birthright. This estate had been in her father's family for generations, and although it hadn't housed a happy family in a very long time, she intended to change that. In the last few years, something had been calling her. A yearning to put right the hurts of the past, to find the old self she'd fled from. Her mother's unexpected death had been a cruel blow to her search, but Christo wasn't going to stop that journey with his confident words and dollar bills.

The solution was simple. "I intend to keep the house, but Stella can stay, of course. It's so huge that there's always plenty to do here. I'll buy your half and everything can be settled."

His look hardened and the confidence oozing from him funneled through her. "As I said, I don't want your money. What I want is this house for my mother's retirement. Not a house for her to keep working in. I'll pay you three times its worth to see that happens. You can buy yourself a permanent place in New York and never feel tied to Brentwood Bay again."

Ruby sat straighter, her shoulders tightening. He was telling her what to do and where to live now? "I *won't* be selling my share, Christo. I grew up in this house, it's part of my heritage, and even though I haven't spent much time here recently, it's more important to me than you understand. Your mother can stay here without working for as long as she wants. God knows she deserves it after being such a wonderful companion to my mother. Whether I spend most of my time in New York or here, Stella will always be welcome in this house." Light relief danced through her chest as the idea blossomed. "Yes, I'd *love* to think of her here. It'll be perfect for both of us."

And my precious baby.

She put a hand to her trembling lips. There was a time Stella Mantazis had been like a second mother to her, and now that her own mother was gone, she couldn't think of anyone more perfect to share her house—or her baby —with.

"Not good enough." His stare held stark irritation. "Now's the time for my mother to be taken care of and cherished, not put up as some sort of charity case lodger. She'll live in this house as its owner, nothing less."

The weight of his determination and the events of the last few weeks drilled into her. Now was not the time to be having this discussion. "This house belongs to me and future generations of Flemings. It's where I'm going to stay." She stood.

"And where I'll stay, too."

Blood changed direction in her veins. "I beg your pardon?"

He moved from the chair and pushed himself to his full height, determination flaring across his features. "Your mother spoke of one condition in her will."

Her lips dried, but she forced the words out. "And what's that?"

"The first person to leave forfeits their share." He picked up a suitcase in each hand. "If you're staying, Ruby, then you can bet I'm staying too."

2

Wet blonde hair hung like a heavy veil down Ruby's back, her luscious curves hidden beneath the towel. The white bikini top cradled perfect breasts, but everything else was sheathed tight.

Lifting her chin, she spoke slowly, her voice hollow. "You are *not* staying here."

Christo pulled his gaze to her shadowed face and focused on the tempting bow of her lips. "It's not an ideal situation, granted," he said. "But I'm sure you can appreciate that I'd be foolish to void my claim from the outset."

The delicate skin on her cheeks paled. "You mean I can't move out while this is sorted or I'll have no claim either?"

"Exactly."

She frowned and shook her head. It was unfortunate he had to do this now, only days after Antonia's funeral, but he had no choice. Either he staked his claim or he'd lose this place, and he wouldn't let that happen. He'd failed to show strength, to fight for his rights here once before.

Never again.

He could've bought his mother her choice of a dozen

houses, one or two even grander than the Fleming Estate, but this was where she was happy. And, as his mother wasn't interested in his money, it was all he had to offer her.

Chemotherapy as a teenager had denied him the chance to provide her with a grandchild, and her unspoken sorrow that she'd never be a yiayia fired his determination to provide her some happiness in her autumn years. It might only be bricks and mortar to him, but this house was where his mother belonged and where she'd be looked after for the rest of her life. Ruby didn't really want the house. She'd settled in New York. This was an act to spite him, just as she'd refused to stand up for him all those years ago. Ruby's parting shot then, that she'd just been using him, lent the final evidence for that. She'd been lying about the way she felt about him all along just to shock her father.

She wouldn't dictate his family's life again. Nobody would. Ever.

He picked up his luggage and nodded toward the house. "After you."

Ruby stood rigid. "Can't this wait until tomorrow? Until I've had a chance to speak to my mom's lawyer?" She folded her arms, pushing her breasts higher so that the delicate silver links of her necklace disappeared into the dip she created. "Until I've spoken to *my* lawyer."

"I'm not prepared to take the risk that my failure to move in tonight might jeopardize my claim. Are you?"

Her nostrils moved, and as her chest rose, the necklace disappeared further. "No."

Glancing around the vast grounds, he shrugged a shoulder. "At the very least, you won't have to stay here on your own."

A rush of air escaped her parted lips. "I've been living on my own in one of the busiest cities in the world. I can manage." She shot him a look, but when he caught the flash in her fiery blue eyes, he only smiled. Indignant, she pulled the towel tighter and walked into the house as he followed.

The sight in front of him caused blood to pump harder through his body—her bottom swaying beneath the towel, the delicate dip of skin between her shoulder blades as she walked. Seeing her like this after ten years caused an unexpectedly intense memory of holding her close, until the result of that intimacy had slammed into him. Losing focus when he was around Ruby Fleming caused chaos and destruction in his own life and the lives of the people he held dear. He'd always prioritize that memory over the first.

They reached the cavernous entrance hall and he turned to her. "When you've changed, we'll talk." Goosebumps traveled over her skin. "I presume you're in an upstairs suite, so I'll take the rooms in the new extension."

She chewed her lip. "Which new rooms?"

He tilted his head to see her face better. "Antonia had a new suite built. The decorating isn't complete yet, but I believe it's habitable. She wanted my mother to move in when her arthritis made it difficult to manage in the housekeeper's apartment. You haven't seen it?"

A shadow passed across Ruby's face. He knew she hadn't been back often, but the fact she hadn't even discussed this with her mom surprised him. Maybe she'd told the truth when she'd said she knew nothing about the will. Antonia had obviously never revealed any of the secrets she'd kept from Ruby, not the least that she'd been blackmailed by Ruby's father.

"No, I haven't seen it. I only arrived the day before the funeral, and I couldn't stay here because there was no one to let me in." The satiny skin at her throat became tight with a swallow, and he considered how it might feel should he brush a finger there. “My first chance to arrange a locksmith was this afternoon,” she said. “If you know about new rooms then by all means go ahead.” She waved a hand toward the downstairs wing and began to climb the stairs. “I’m getting changed.”

He watched her go, appreciating the sway of her hips as she ascended, her bare feet reaching for each new step. After the lesson she’d taught him when they were young, he might know her for who and what she was, but there was no denying one thing—she still made his heart clench.

When he’d deposited his luggage and showered, Christo headed to the wine cellar and chose a vintage Pinot Noir. It had been a long day, a few long days in a row since he’d boarded his jet in Athens where he’d been holidaying and flown virtually non-stop to arrive here.

His muscles sagged. If he didn’t relax before going to bed he’d never kick the jet lag, and the focus he needed for this transaction could be compromised. He’d missed the funeral, unfortunately. It would’ve been good to pay Antonia the respect she deserved, but at least he was here now to claim the house, as she would’ve wanted.

It wouldn’t take him long to persuade Ruby to part with her share. By all accounts, she had a hectic life in publishing in New York. She’d probably put up a little fight for old times’ sake, but she’d give in and see logic eventually. No reason why he couldn’t enjoy a little challenge on the way to achieving his goal—the way her eyes blazed in indignation each time his logic rattled her was mesmerizing.

He heard her footsteps on the stairs and removed another glass from the shelf in the kitchen.

“Glass of red?” He swung his gaze in her direction and tried to deflect the sucker punch that seized his insides when he saw her.

A turquoise dress, tight around her chest, flowed out across her body, hardly hinting at her shape beneath. Her blonde hair curled loose and wild around her shoulders except for a strand tucked behind a perfect ear hung with a simple gold hoop. Standing straight on heels with her bag over her shoulder, her skin was honeyed bronze from her Italian mother, her irises sparkling cobalt blue from her father. She took his breath away.

Christo shook himself.

Focus.

He didn't do weak. Wouldn't let this loss of attention, this slip in control when he was around Ruby, happen again. It was his untamed physical reaction to her that had clouded his judgment in the past and led to disaster for him and his mother. Ruby Fleming had been his Achilles heel, but he was a different man now. A man whose determination to win at all costs had been galvanized by her father's humiliating decree, and Ruby's bare-faced refusal to stand up for him. When she'd angrily followed him after her father's allegations, she'd shouted at him, accusing him of using her to climb some social ladder. *"I was convenient for you?"* she'd cried. "*Well, guess what? You were convenient for me too. I wanted to shock Dad, show him I wasn't his little girl anymore. I think it worked, don't you?"*

Yes, it was weakness that had caused him to believe Ruby's feelings for him were genuine. Trusting her had been his biggest mistake.

"I see you've made yourself at home." Her chin nudged a fraction higher and her glossy lips parted. "Don't get too comfortable. I've left a message for my lawyer in New York. As soon as she wakes I'm sure she'll have something to say about your *claims.*"

He held up the glass and responded to her jibe with a

slow smile. "This is what we've been drinking for Sunday lunches. It's from one of my vineyards in Napa. Earthy."

"Sunday lunches?" She rolled a lip between her teeth as her eyebrows rose. "Here?"

Relaxing against the marble counter, he nodded. "My mom was worried Antonia wasn't eating enough, so she cooked Greek lamb and potatoes every Sunday."

"Oh."

At the lost look on her face, he paused, but if she was to understand her mom's will she needed to know the reality about the people she left behind. "Antonia invited me along one Sunday shortly after your father died and it became a tradition for the three of us. There's plenty more where this came from."

He cleared his throat and lounged further against the counter. "You're going out?"

She tilted her chin a fraction. "Yes."

"Where?" He took a mouthful of wine and let the liquid warm on his tongue.

Her jaw moved side to side before she spoke, and her fingers curled around the strap of her bag. "My uncle's restaurant."

"Ah, Lorenzo has a great reputation in town. *Felice* is a fine establishment."

Her voice was thin as her cheeks blanched. "You know my uncle? He didn't get on with my father, so he never came to the house when we were young..." When he didn't reply she paused. "He insisted that he cook for me tonight, and I don't have the stomach for staying in."

Holding his gaze, he lowered his voice. "You realize that if you go out alone now you'll forfeit your claim on the house."

Her mouth parted and the tip of her tongue dampened

her lips. "I'll only be an hour or two. It's important. It's family."

Passing her the glass of wine, he spoke smoothly. "The conditions of the will dictate that the person remaining here wins the house outright. Technically, I'll be here, and you'll have left, possibly for good. If we're both out, no problem. Both in, no problem. But if you choose to go out on your own tonight, you've left. And I'll have sent your luggage after you." He shrugged. "You won't have a claim."

A soft sound left Ruby's lips. "Surely such a ridiculous rule would be thrown out in court."

"Possibly." He watched a rose blush sweep up her neck. "But I'd be prepared to fight through those courts. Appeal if I had to. I'm sure you wouldn't want your hard-earned money squandered over something so easily avoided."

Ruby shook her head and blonde ringlets brushed her skin. "Why? Why would Mom make that a requirement?"

He leaned harder against the counter and trained his gaze on the bloom of her cheeks. "Your mother couldn't give me the house outright, Ruby. She wanted you to benefit financially from its sale, but she wanted to ensure I had first option over it for my mother. You'd made it clear you had no desire to return to Brentwood Bay, and she didn't want to see the house slip into the hands of strangers."

She swung her gaze to his face and something kicked in his chest. She looked lost and vulnerable, and part of him wanted to help her understand what had obviously come as an enormous shock. "Having this condition means you have to stay and see this through. Negotiate. We both do."

Ruby shook her head again, her tone distant as she pushed the wine glass back toward him, untouched. "Thank you, but I'm sure it'll all be cleared up after I speak to my lawyer in the morning. In the meantime, you can go and we can simply say you were here all night. No one needs to know."

He slung a hand in his pants pocket. He'd have to trust her for that to work, something he was unwilling to do. She'd used him once. Never again.

It might seem harsh to push her on this first night, but he couldn't let the opportunity go when he'd come so close to getting what he must have. "Ruby, you're forgetting that I need this property. I won't gamble on half-baked ideas or lies. I'll do what it takes to win. And that means sleeping under this roof, starting tonight."

She pulled her shoulders back. "This house has been passed down my father's line and should've come to his only child. I'll appeal. Surely I can appeal and have you thrown out."

He scraped a hand across his chin, and the pink smudge on her cheeks deepened. "Ah, yes, have me thrown out. I suppose you could. But that's what got us here in the first place, isn't it?"

Did she remember the night his father had caught them together? Did she ever wonder what it was like for him to be banished from his home? The sense of failure he would *never* let himself experience again?

Cancer had been a tough battle for a teenager, as was living a life without a father, but what Ruby had done to him, the way she'd failed to stand by him when her father had ordered him out, then claimed that kissing him had all been an act to shock, had been the greatest lesson of his life. Only the strong survive. He'd never let himself be anything but strong or successful since.

Dismay swept across her face at mention of their past before she hurriedly glanced at her wrist, and color returned to her bleached cheeks. Christo dipped to hear her words. "My uncle's expecting me."

He leaned back and took another mouthful of wine, swirled it in his mouth, and swallowed. "Go to him, of course. It's important you're with family now. But I can't let you lose so easily. It wouldn't be fair." He paused as he watched her face change. "I'll come with you so neither of us wins this round." He threw her a lazy smile. "I'm hungry anyway."

Her eyes flashed. "You're enjoying this, aren't you?"

Something dislodged in his chest. This wasn't pleasant, wasn't fun. Of all people, he didn't like having to ask Ruby Fleming for something. That she thought he was enjoying it cut deep. She obviously knew nothing of his heart and mind. And why would she, when every one of her whispered words back then had been as empty as her heart the day he left?

She swung her bag over her shoulder, then met his gaze and swallowed slowly. "If there's no other way, then you'll need to come with me. But this crazy arrangement will be sorted out tomorrow and then we'll both be free. Whatever she meant, I'm certain Mom didn't intend for me to be imprisoned here."

His mouth pulled in a grim smile. "Sorting things tomorrow is fine by me."

Ruby was determined to fight this, but until she came to see that she didn't need this house, that in letting it go she could move on with her life and let go of her past, he'd be staying right here. Enjoying the sight of her for breakfast, lunch, and dinner.

"Are you cold? I'll put the hard top up." Christo's husky voice traveled the small distance between them in the convertible, but Ruby kept her eyes trained on the diamond flash of the town's lights. Ahead lay Brentwood Bay Harbor, and, on its edges, her uncle's restaurant. The evening breeze tugged at her hair, flicking it about her shoulders—and accentuated the intoxicating scent of Christo so close.

"No, I'm fine, thanks." She rubbed her arms, elbows tight against her body. It was time she told him about her baby, about why he couldn't buy her out of her heritage. He wouldn't be the first to know, though. She couldn't allow that. She was only fifteen weeks along and had been waiting to tell her mom, praying it would be the beginning of a new relationship for them.

Placing her palm lightly on her belly, she resolved to tell her aunt and uncle, her only remaining family, before she told Christo, and then this nightmare would be over. Given their past he might be motivated to fight her, but he wouldn't deny her precious baby its heritage. Her heart was heavy. It would mean Stella would need to move out, but Christo wouldn't hear of an alternative solution.

A headache bit deep behind her eyes. All she wanted was to curl up in her own bed and sleep. Or sob. For the mother she'd lost, for the baby she'd do anything to protect.

"Strange being back?" His voice carried across the breeze.

Turning her head, she let her gaze flit across his brooding profile.

Stranger than he could imagine. Being so close to him, as a woman now instead of the teenager he'd known. She shifted against the warm leather cushioning her skin as memories of being close to him flared within. The sultry evening he'd drawn her into his arms in the summerhouse before telling her he was in love with her. She moistened her lips. "A little. Even though I've been in New York, I only travel a small area between my apartment and work. Somehow I'd forgotten the way everything's so spread out here."

The corner of his mouth kicked up, white teeth flashing in the muted blue light from the dashboard. "Brentwood Bay's very small. A village compared to where you've come from."

Her gaze moved to his hands gripping the sleek steering wheel. Expensive European cars were common enough in New York, but she didn't often ride in one. What had he been doing to become so successful? The car, the Rolex, the vineyards, the offer for her half of the house at three times the value. He'd obviously been rewarded well for something.

He turned the car into the parking lot outside her uncle's restaurant, raised the hard roof, and killed the engine. All the air in the car seemed to be sucked out, and her chest tightened. She reached for her seatbelt, but he stayed still, the power of his rigid body humming in the close air. Curious, she twisted back to see why he wasn't moving.

"I would've come to your mom's funeral, Ruby. If I'd known in time." His tone was low and smoky. "I always did what I could for Antonia." His fist stayed curled around the emergency brake, inches from her thigh, and she took a moment to steady herself at the tenderness of his tone. He'd cared for her mother. She'd always known that.

"I'm sorry you didn't have more notice. The executor of the estate made the funeral arrangements as I was traveling back. I didn't think to ask him to contact you, and I didn't know your mom was in Greece." Her throat constricted, chest hollow as she looked up to his face. His look unhinged her.

Grief painted his features before he seemed to pull himself together, and his sadness at her mother's death was buried again. "If we can work this out between us, I'd prefer it," he said.

"You don't want lawyers involved?" She shifted in her seat. Maybe they could resolve this without too much trouble.

"Lawyers and I don't always see eye to eye, but it's not that." Unlocked resentment seethed beneath his smooth surface.

She clutched her hands in her lap. "There's something I need to tell you that'll change your mind about claiming the house. I need to talk to my uncle and aunt about it first, but we won't need lawyers."

For a second, a muscle jumped at his jaw before he turned his charcoal stare to her. "*Nothing* you say will stop me claiming my mother's home. We'll finalize it sooner rather than later."

She bit down on her lip. There was no point discussing it now—not until he had all the facts. He'd know tomorrow. Surely he'd stop fighting her then?

He leaned an elbow on the window frame, his jaw tipped higher. "I'd prefer to get this resolved before certain people get wind of it."

Did he have a girlfriend he was sheltering from this situation? Ruby knew nothing about this Christo—he could have a wife for all she knew. Before she could help herself, she asked, "Certain people?"

He gripped the steering wheel. "The media. I've a strict policy of keeping my private life private, and there are too many people depending on me for their livelihoods for my business to be rocked by ill-informed gossip. I won't have photographers camping out on our doorstep, finding scandal where there isn't any. You can be sure if lawyers are involved some Personal Assistant will talk to some executive and it'll be all over the town."

Our doorstep. He'd said the words as naturally as if he'd said he'd wanted a cup of coffee.

A thorn of curiosity buried itself in her mind. "Why would the media be interested in you?" Had he been in scandals or relationships with high profile women? Or was his success linked to something public?

"I have deals in the pipeline. Contracts that can't be jeopardized. Important engagements I can't miss, organizations that depend on my reputation for their success. This needs to be resolved as soon as possible so we're both free to get on with our lives, and my mother can move back to her home."

She tilted her head in acknowledgement. "And you won't be free to do those things when you're stuck in the house with me."

"Exactly—and you need to return to New York. It makes sense that after you've spoken to your mother's lawyer tomorrow we'll resolve this."

A noisy group of people walked past the car and headed into the restaurant, Italian music playing louder and then softer as they opened and shut the large oak door. By the number of tables on the seaward balcony, her uncle Lorenzo certainly seemed to be doing well. The last she'd heard, his business had been floundering, so it was nice to see someone in her family finding some joy in life.

Thinking about her uncle and his love for food and good company called up an image of Christo's mother. The sweet, warm memory of Stella Mantazis's cuddles, her comforting food, and her gently scolding tongue drifted around Ruby like a whisper. "Does your mom know what you're doing?" She couldn't imagine Stella demanding that Christo fight her for the house. It wasn't in her nature.

"No." He glanced away and back to her again, his face a stony mask. "She'd only want to live in the house if she truly believed you didn't want it."

Ruby clutched her hands tighter and took a deeper breath. "But if she were to live there with me the way she's always done... Stella will understand why I have to keep the house. She understands about love and memories. When I speak to her—"

Every muscle in Christo's body seemed to jump to attention, and the air between them arced. "You will *not* speak to my mother, Ruby."

The beat of blood grew stronger in her tightly laced fingers, and she strained across the darkened space to read him. "Why not?"

"My mother won't know any of this. From *anyone*." His words, short and sharp like bullets, peppered her skin. "As far as she's concerned this will be her house outright, you'll have no interest in it at all. I won't have her working any more, or staying with you as little more than a charity case. We'll sign an agreement, and then you can return home."

Ruby reached for her bag with a trembling hand. He might be comfortable telling other people what to do, but he would *not* speak to her that way. Struggling to keep her voice steady, she twisted around and fixed him with a stare. "Right now I'm going to have a meal with the only remaining members of my family. Join me if you wish, but do *not* order me around."

Grabbing the handle, she wrenched the door open and stepped out of the car. As she made her way across the parking lot, the slam of his door and the beat of his footfalls thudded behind her. In seconds he was beside her, and she turned her face to him.

"I don't get it, Ruby." His voice was low and sultry. "You've lived in another city for years. You rarely, if ever, visit here. You've flicked off your past as if it were an irritation. Why not take my money and go, get back to your life on the other side of the country without any fuss?"

She was bursting to tell him the reason, to explain everything, but she desperately wanted the first people to hear about her baby to be family. Family members who were on the other side of that door.

She dampened her dry lips. "Can we wait a few more minutes to have this conversation? Let me speak to my uncle first."

He surveyed her for a moment, then inclined his head and opened the door for her.

3

From across the restaurant, her uncle Lorenzo spotted Ruby and came hurrying over, his pink face beaming. Her knees weakened at the sight of someone who loved her, someone who cared about what she was going through, and the emotion of the last few weeks surged in her chest. She couldn't wait to tell Lorenzo he was going to be a great uncle.

Throwing his arms wide, Lorenzo's face broke into a smile, his bushy gray eyebrows shooting up his forehead. "Ruby, sweetheart, come through. We must be together tonight and remember your beautiful mother, God rest her soul." His dark eyes twinkled as he tilted his head to one side. "And Christo! Are you two here together?"

Suddenly the warm touch of Christo's hand was on her back and every nerve ending leapt to attention. The promise of that touch was something she'd carried inside her, *dreamed* about for years, but now it felt secret and full of power, something she didn't know how to interpret.

"Wonderful to see you, Christo," Lorenzo said. "I was

hoping you'd come by this month and see how well the new kitchen's operating. You were right. It was better to go with the triple ventilation system. It works perfectly with those Italian ovens you imported."

The ground shifted beneath her feet, and Ruby stepped out of Christo's touch. As the two men chatted like old friends, her head swirled. Not only had Christo spent God knows how many months manipulating her mother into giving him a share of the house, it seemed he'd infiltrated the rest of her family too. What was his game? Was it the house he wanted, or did he have some plan of revenge against her?

"This is the savior of *Felice*." Lorenzo thumped Christo on the back while Ruby steadied herself. "He rescued us from our darkest hour! And for that he gets free Parmigiana for the rest of his life! Come, you two. I'll find you the best table in the house."

"Uncle Lorenzo," she said with a staying hand on his arm. "There's something I need to tell you. Is Aunt Sophia here?"

"Your aunt and cousins will drop by later, my love. Now you need to eat. There will be plenty of time for talk." He held her hand and began moving.

Heart falling, Ruby followed her uncle across the restaurant, weaving among tables bursting with happy people.

She'd been so focused on telling her family about the pregnancy and finding some joy on the day she'd been confronted by the terms of the will. Yet first she'd have to sit through a meal with Christo, a man who surprised her at every turn. A man she couldn't trust. Would the news of her pregnancy be enough to deter him? If he'd charmed his way this deep, this ruthlessly into her family, where would he stop?

They arrived at a table overlooking yachts in the marina, and Lorenzo pulled her into a tight hug. "Little Ruby. Oh, little Ruby, we've missed you, and now that your mama's gone you must come back and be with people who love you."

Ruby clung to her mother's brother and she trembled. No one really knew the reason she'd stayed away. Only she'd known of her mother's secret long-term affair that had caused her family to implode. Although it was too late to forgive her mom to her face, she'd done it in her heart. The release of disappointment and hurt was like manacles being liberated from her soul. A week too late.

So much in her future now depended upon reclaiming the identity she'd lost when she left this town. Her home. To be the best mom she could be to the life inside her, Ruby owed it to herself and to her baby to stay away from the influences that had robbed her of her self-worth then. Influences like Christo Mantazis's deception.

Lifting lashes heavy with tears, she saw Christo watching her, the creases at the edge of his mouth deeper, his hand resting on a chair.

"The house specialty for you two tonight," Lorenzo said as he stepped away and rubbed his black chef's jacket sleeve across his eyes. "I'll send Giancarlo over with some Mantazis wine to get you started."

Christo held out her chair and she sat, pulling every muscle tight and swallowing away more tears. She watched him as he nodded to people at a number of different tables, folded himself into a chair, and laid the crisp white napkin across his knees.

Her fingers curled around a cool water glass and she waited until he looked at her. "What's going on, Christo?"

He turned toward the bar, lifted his chin to a waiter, then swung his attention back to her. "Going on?"

"Why are you so hand in glove with Lorenzo? Did you think pulling the whole of my family into the trap to gain the house would work? Lorenzo and Sophia want me to come back to Brentwood Bay. You heard him."

She glanced over to the kitchen door where her uncle had disappeared. "They'll be shocked to learn what Mom's done, what you're trying to do."

He rested an elbow on the tablecloth and paused before touching two fingers to his lips, riveting her with his stare. "Your uncle Lorenzo's gambling was out of hand. He could've lost the restaurant, his house, your cousins' college funds... I bought the building and renovated the restaurant, that's all. He pulled himself out of debt with the quality of his cooking."

She scanned the crowded dining room for her beloved aunt and cousins before letting her gaze settle back on his face. She didn't want to believe what Christo had said, but in her heart she knew he was telling the truth. Lorenzo had always liked to take risks. "He was in that much trouble? It was good of you to help out."

He didn't acknowledge the praise, merely held her gaze, the flickering light of the candle intensifying the spark in his stare.

Her lips touched her glass, the cool condensation soothing the hot tangle of confusion inside. "But why *you*? For someone in *my* family?" Christo despised her family for the way her father had refused to ever allow him back in the house.

He shrugged in an uncaring, what-does-it-matter way. "I like Italian food."

Pausing, she sucked in her cheeks, and was captivated by

the flickering heat from his stare. "Why, Christo? I need to know." Her heart dropped. "Is this about revenge? Proving a point? Is your pride still so pricked from my father sending you away that you have to fight me now?"

His gaze intensified at the accusation. "Your uncle was good to me once. When I'd been forbidden to set foot back in my home, Lorenzo would let my mother and me sit in his restaurant for hours, drinking free coffee and catching up in a way we never could in our home again. After the way I'd been treated, I appreciated it."

A picture reel of those stolen moments whirled through her head as she shifted the napkin on her knee. What must it have been like for him, arranging secret meetings with his mother, miles from the only home he'd known? She thought of being separated from her own baby and her chest ached. She stroked the soft fabric across her belly. Yet Christo had created the situation that had led to his estrangement from the Fleming Estate. He'd denied it back then, when she'd gone after him and asked if he'd been with other women, if he was only with her because of who she was.

When you're ready to explain yourself, I'll be waiting, she'd said as he hurried from the house. When he didn't look back she'd wanted to hurt him too and said she'd only been using him to shock her father. Still he'd kept on walking.

He hadn't come to find her until today. And although the sting of his silence then had lessened over the years, the pain she'd felt at his refusal to explain himself, to stay and face the consequences of his actions, was still within reach.

But why would her uncle have offered him some refuge? An unsavory thought unraveled in her mind, and her pulse began to drum at her temples. "Did my mother arrange for you to meet at her brother's restaurant all those years ago?"

He didn't flinch. "Yes. And we were grateful for it. My mother never forgot the support Antonia gave us, which was why my mother would do anything for her. And why Antonia would hate to think of you denying my mother her home now."

Her jaw clenched as disappointment and hurt filled her throat. If her mother had wanted to support Christo like that, after what he'd done...

Her death grip on the napkin resting on her lap eased and she sat carefully back. That episode in her life was all behind her now—all the pain both her mother and Christo had caused. Still, she couldn't help but dig deeper.

"Did Mom ask you to help Lorenzo later?"

He leaned back in his chair and spoke with steely confidence again. "Your mother was distressed that her only family left here was falling apart. Before he died, your father screwed down every income stream, so she had very little. She couldn't offer Lorenzo assistance. I was happy to help after everything she'd done for me."

She shook her head, trying to make sense of everything she'd learned today. "My mother had no access to her own money? Why would Dad do that?"

The waiter appeared with a bottle of wine, and Ruby watched as he poured a small measure of the velvet red liquid into Christo's glass. As if valuing an ancient piece of art, Christo regarded the wine, swirled it in the enormous bowl, then bowed his head and inhaled.

A shock of unbidden desire flooded her. His glossy black hair, the seductive set of broad shoulders. So much about him hadn't changed. He'd taken as much care over her once —his long, languorous kisses. She sat back quickly in her chair as her body thrummed.

With a sharp nod, he spoke to the waiter. "Fine. My

Napa winemakers outdid themselves with that vintage. Some for my companion. I'm driving."

Another waiter arrived and placed a selection of tiny treats in front of them, and the aroma of garlic and herbs reminded her she hadn't eaten since lunch. There was a precious little life depending on her making the right choices now, to nourish her mind *and* her body. She picked up a delicate piece of toasted bread topped with a slice of deep red tomato and put it to her lips.

"So," Christo said, not moving for the food but focusing directly on her. "Why have you been away so long?"

She bit down, but not even the rich flavors could distract her from the intensity of his stare. When she'd finished chewing, she brushed her fingers on her napkin. "I've had a good career in magazine publishing. Plenty of opportunities. I've been very lucky."

"You weren't hiding from anything?" His voice held deceptive casualness.

She took a sip of water, hoping he wouldn't notice she hadn't touched the wine. "What do you mean?"

"You weren't avoiding me or your mother?"

Biting her lip, she swallowed again. He wouldn't slip under her skin that easily. "Christo, I left here when I was eighteen. If I was to think of you while I was away, it would've been to thank someone for making me understand your real intentions toward me." If she'd never discovered his duplicity, she could've ended up married to this man, thinking he was as deeply in love with her as she was with him, yet all the time being played for a fool.

"Someone like your father?"

She tensed at his tone. At his implied criticism. "At least someone was looking out for me back then. Telling me the truth."

His ebony stare flamed. "*I* was looking out for you."

Heat poured into her cheeks at the sensuality and power in his voice, and she turned her head as the woman at the next table made a loud noise.

"Ah, Christo!" The woman scraped her chair back on the wooden floor and glided to the table. A voluminous silk sleeve flicked Ruby in the face as Christo stood and the woman leaned in to be kissed on both cheeks.

"Marguerite. What a surprise." His voice was low and measured.

Ruby glanced at the woman's companion at the next table. It was as if a thundercloud had rolled across his features.

Christo gestured to Ruby. "May I introduce—"

"We're *so* delighted you've agreed to appear at the charity ball on Friday." She spoke in syrup-coated tones over his introduction. "It's *much* more than we'd hoped for."

Christo pulled at the cuff of his cream shirt, his spine arrow-straight. "My PA, Patrice, deals with the details. I'll do what I can."

The woman leaned a little closer to him, her hip blocking Ruby as if she were some unpleasant table decoration. "I will look forward to it, as will the other girls on the committee. We were only saying the other day how marvelous it was to see you in the society pages last week doing what you do *so well*." Ruby shifted in her seat and saw Christo lean back as the woman dragged the tip of a meaty tongue across her full, top lip.

"Thank you," he said graciously. "I do hope you enjoy your meal tonight." He gestured toward her table and her thunderhead of a husband.

Ten years had passed, but still the ladies of Brentwood Bay's millionaire set were swooning over Christo Mantazis.

And he was obviously still giving them what they wanted. An idea formed, a way to ensure this impasse was resolved quickly. Attending a function and leaving her alone would mean he'd forfeit the house. If he was prepared to fight using that ridiculous rule, then so could she. "Your charity ball's in three days?"

The woman turned her cheek in Ruby's direction. "It is. It's become quite the event on the calendar. Invitation only, *naturally*."

"Then I'm sure Mr. Mantazis won't miss it," she said, smiling. "Nothing to keep him away."

"And *you* are?" Marguerite's nostrils flared as her mountainous chest thrust outward. "His PA?"

"No," Ruby said. "Just someone concerned about his timetable."

Christo took a step toward his chair and a smile slid onto the woman's face again. "Such a pleasure, Christo. We've such a *lot* to be grateful to you for. Until Friday." She lifted her hand and waggled her fingers at him before turning, and he sat down with a barely disguised thump.

"So you're going out Friday night." Ruby lifted the water glass to her mouth. "I guess we'll need to come to an agreement before then, or your friend might be disappointed."

"Yes." He poured water into his glass. "Where were we?"

Ruby couldn't help watching the way the woman's husband spoke to her through gritted teeth and the way Marguerite kept looking at Christo from under her bushy lashes. *A charmer*, her father had called him. *A social-climbing, devious charmer*. "You were telling me how you were looking out for me when you used me."

His hand froze in mid-air. "That's not how it was, Ruby."

"You weren't with other women?" She tore a piece of ciabatta and put it in her mouth, all the time holding his gaze. Her head told her to leave this, but a slow grind in her chest forced her on. If she'd wanted to return to Brentwood Bay to search for her lost identity, then perhaps questioning the person who had a hand in taking it from her was a start. "You weren't trawling yacht clubs and resorts to make the right connections? Gain new heights, so to speak?"

He leaned closer, the neck muscles beneath his collar cording as the lines around his eyes deepened. "I had been friends with other women, but that was before you and I became involved. As soon as I realized the connection we had, I didn't look at anyone else. I changed when we got together."

It still hurt deep inside that she'd been one of many, and that he was now offering her an implausible excuse of having changed. "Sure, you changed. You'd just hooked me, someone whose father was richer than all of those women put together. If you'd turned your focus solely on me it wasn't for fidelity's sake, but because my connections were more attractive."

He shook his head in two swift movements, jaw set solid. "I see you're as willing to believe the worst about me now as you were then."

"I gave you an opportunity to explain yourself then. You couldn't get away from me fast enough." She sipped her water, steadying her trembling hand. "And it seems you've got the same trail of admirers you had all those years ago."

He lifted one shoulder and shrugged lazily. "It's part of the business."

"And what business would that be? You own a winery, I believe."

"The vineyards are a hobby. The gyms and health resorts are where I started. Now I'm an entrepreneur."

"I see."

He picked up a piece of bread, then paused and met her eyes again. "Your father did me one favor."

"What was that?"

"Nothing spurs a man to greater success than the pursuit of the truth and the hunger to win when he's been wronged. Your father set me free when he threw me out of the house. He made me hungry, determined. Opened my eyes about what and who to avoid in my life."

"And what and who might that be?"

A muscle pulsed on his jaw. "Temptation and tricksters."

A waiter placed enormous plates in front of them and Ruby looked down. Was he saying she still tempted him? Or that he didn't trust her?

There was something trapped in this man in front of her, something crouching, ready to pounce. And, although she wished it wasn't so, part of her wanted to find out what that something was.

"So what do you think, Stephanie? What are my options?"

Ruby transferred the cell to her other ear very early the next morning and listened carefully for her lawyer's response to the story she'd just told her.

"We'll know more when I've received details from your mother's lawyer, but leaving a half share to the son of one's housekeeper does sound pretty left field," her lawyer said. "I've seen far stranger things in other wills, though. There's a good possibility it's legitimate. A court battle could become protracted, so I'd push for an informal negotiation if you can."

"But what about having to share the house while we sort it out? Is that legal?" Ruby eased herself from the bed and padded across to the enormous sash window. She'd opened it when she'd woken and a sweet breeze drifted in from the garden.

"That part does sound more unusual. You'll be given a copy of the will when you meet with your mother's solicitor today and can verify then if it's legitimate. I'd imagine if he's making it up then it's a simple matter of issuing him with a trespass notice."

"And if it *is* in the will? What can I do then?"

"You'll need to decide how much you want to fight for the house. If he's offered you three times what it's worth then you might want to consider that offer. It's a good one."

Ruby hadn't told her lawyer she was pregnant, or how much keeping the house meant to her. She'd wanted some cold, hard clarity on all of this and her lawyer was certainly giving it to her.

"One thing you'll need to consider is whether you want a drawn out battle over this. Too many times I've seen issues over wills carry on for years and all of the assets liquidated to pay court costs."

That wouldn't be happening, Ruby thought. No way would she let this house and everything in it be frittered away. Some way, some how, she and Christo would come to an agreement today. All she knew right now was that she wouldn't be the one leaving here.

A heavy buzz of fatigue dragged through Ruby's body as she carefully tugged open her bedroom door thirty minutes later.

She'd been texting one of her best friends, Kirin, who'd

been at her mom's funeral, and they'd made plans to meet up soon. She'd only told Kirin part of what had transpired since the funeral, seeing Christo and him wanting to buy her out. She hadn't said that he'd been given half the house too. Her friends and colleagues wouldn't believe the real story of what had been happening with Christo—it still sounded like a far-fetched fantasy in her own mind. Kirin had wanted to know if she was thinking about staying longer in Brentwood Bay. By the end of today she hoped she'd have an answer.

A soft curtain of early morning light made it easy enough to see as she made her way down the staircase to the front door—she'd just go down to the summerhouse before she had to see Christo again. It was where she'd found comfort when she was confused as a teenager, where she'd sit and soothe herself by making jewelry.

As she moved forward, a floorboard squeaked beneath her feet. The same floorboard, the same squeak as when she'd been an oblivious, innocent child running up and down these stairs. She remembered those weekends she'd stayed with her grandparents, before they'd passed away and she'd moved in here with her own parents. Back then, being in the house with Gran and Grandpa had felt as if she'd been wrapped in love, soaked in it. Something inside her shifted.

From the glassed atrium she looked across Bentwood Bay and felt the pull of her birthplace. When she'd come back in such a hurry for her mother's funeral, she hadn't made the decision whether she'd be back here for good. Being here now, preparing for the birth of her baby, was the chance to forge a fresh destiny. A new positivity bubbled through her. She'd need to return to New York briefly to wrap up her job and sell her apartment, but the prospect of a whole new life here with her baby would ease the pain of cutting those ties.

Pausing as she neared the bottom of the stairs, she checked over the banister. She didn't want to talk to Christo yet. In private, she'd told her aunt and uncle about her baby last night and of course they'd been thrilled. Now she wanted to see her mother's lawyer to find out how that affected the terms of the will. When she knew, she'd speak to Christo.

As her bare foot reached for the final step a sudden thought grabbed her and she glanced toward the kitchen door. Her bag with the house keys in it—it still sat on the counter where she'd left it after returning from the restaurant. Getting away from Christo's constant, confusing presence last night had been her only goal when they'd arrived home. She hadn't been in the summerhouse since she'd been back, and she knew it would be locked.

Moving as carefully as a cat, she put her palm against the cool wood and pushed open the kitchen door. As she tiptoed inside, her heart fell to her heels.

"Good morning." Christo swiveled from where he stood behind the counter looking freshly showered and impossibly relaxed, a glass of water at his lips. Damp hair shone against his face, the stubble from late yesterday replaced by smooth, bronzed skin that glowed. His cheek curved in a smoldering grin. "If you'd been up earlier you could've come for a run. It's a great day out there."

Ruby drew the tip of her tongue across her lips, and her heart skipped inside her ribcage. "You've run and showered already? Did you leave the grounds?"

He let out a soft chuckle. "I guess you'll never know."

A splash of moisture dampened his chin, and Ruby stared at the spot. As he lowered the glass, he wiped the drop away, slow and firm with the back of his hand. "Take a seat. I'll make breakfast."

Grasping her bag, she turned her head, anywhere but in the direction of Christo's mouth, his ruggedly toned body. She spoke quietly. "There won't be anything to eat. I didn't have a chance to go to the grocery store yesterday."

He moved effortlessly about the kitchen, opening drawers before pulling out a bowl. "I had my restaurant supplier drop a few things off before he went to the markets this morning. Our appointment with your mother's lawyer is not until nine-thirty. There's plenty of time."

She glanced from the bag to his face and stumbled on her words. "You're coming?" A knot in the center of her back gripped tight, and she twisted around to knead the spot deep with her fingertips, not quite reaching.

He spoke with his back to her as he opened the fridge. "The first person to leave, remember? But your mother's lawyer wanted me to come in with you today anyway. He agrees mediation's the best and quickest option. Everything could be sorted out by the end of the day if you're agreeable." He didn't stop what he was doing—balancing a tray of eggs and a bunch of herbs on his strong forearm.

A lumpy sigh worked up and down her throat. She could give him a hundred responses, but what was the point in fighting this now? Conserving her energy for the battle in the lawyer's office seemed far more sensible. Besides, she was starving. Now that the morning sickness was gone, she was always hungry first thing.

"Sore back?"

Lifting unwilling eyes to his, she realized she was still trying to work the muscles in her shoulders. Her hand froze as his gaze pinned her.

"I didn't sleep very well, must've pulled a muscle or something." Face heating, her hands dropped to her sides.

"You need a good masseuse, someone to iron out those tense muscles. It can turn into a migraine if you don't fix it quickly enough. I noticed the tension and fatigue in you yesterday."

For a volatile second Ruby imagined him watching her in her bikini, skin exposed, body revealed. How much had he seen? Did he know about the pregnancy?

Her hand fluttered absently to her stomach, then her mind sprinted to the image of his strong hands tending her muscles, how he'd tease them from rigid ropes to supple strands beneath his confident fingers. Her mouth dried and she looked away.

Was he doing this on purpose? Understanding the reaction she still had to him and working to keep her off guard? Being off guard around Christo was not something she intended to do again in this lifetime.

He reached to the rack of pans above his head and his T-shirt rode up, revealing a window of tight stomach muscles and a shadow of dark hair reaching down. So different from the slickly stylish suit he'd worn yesterday—and so tempting.

"I own the best health clubs in Northern Cali." His stomach was hidden once more. "I can arrange for you to see someone after our appointment today. He can even come here. The hot tub on the terrace will be good for you, too." He placed the pan on the gas and flicked the ignition.

Ruby shook her head as if to prove her neck was as loose as a newborn giraffe's, but a crack sent pain shooting upwards. Suddenly she felt lightheaded.

"I will have that seat." She slid onto the familiar kitchen stool as her head throbbed. Butter sizzled in the pan and

Christo broke eggs into a bowl. Her mother's silver espresso pot bubbled on the stove, sending invisible coffee trails through the air.

She rubbed her temples as she watched him, each movement of his powerful body mesmerizing her. "You look as though you know your way around this kitchen well."

He shrugged and pushed a sleeve up. "My mother's kept this kitchen pretty much the same since she arrived as a twenty-five year old." A richly genuine smile painted his features for a second. "Remember when we'd come in here as kids and eat her honey cakes?"

Ruby rested her elbows on the countertop, warm memories of her early childhood drifting from deep within. She let her tongue run along her top lip at the memory of his mother's exquisite cakes. The thought of Stella Mantazis here with Ruby's own child caused a smile to touch her mouth. *That's* what she was going to fight for today.

Christo was whisking the eggs, concentration written on his face. Who was this person in front of her—a man who could change from cold businessman to man-about-the-kitchen in a matter of hours? Was he doing all this to win her over? Charm her? Make her think that after everything that had happened she owed him this house? She tilted her chin. "What does Stella think of you being here with me?"

He beat the eggs, but his sizzling stare stayed hooked on hers.

She nodded, understanding, as he stayed silent and a muscle contracted on his cheek. "She doesn't know, does she? Your mother doesn't know anything about this at all."

He gave the eggs a final beat and poured them into the pan. "She doesn't need to. This will be resolved by the end of the day. She can return with the knowledge that this is all hers, fair and square."

"And you're sure this is what she wants. This house."

Turning from the stove, his gaze pulled her in. "The two places my mother is happiest in the world are Greece and Brentwood Bay. Because I'm here, she wants to be too. And I'll make sure she has everything she wants and all she needs here. This house is one of those things."

Maybe it was the crazy intimacy of the situation, but she wanted to know more. "You're very confident of winning. Is it because you don't like to lose?"

His dark stare sharpened as he turned back to her. "I operate on needs-based logic, not emotion. I need this house for my mother, not because it's grand or in the right position. I could've bought her dozens of houses like that. I need it because it's the only one of its kind. My mother's home. That's why it will be hers. You have your whole lifetime to make yourself another home. My mother doesn't."

He had no idea what the concept of home meant for her. Now was the time to tell him—no more waiting. Ruby stitched a smile to her face and clasped her hands together on the cool countertop. "I need this home too, for the baby I'm carrying. He or she has the right to it."

All was silent while he moved a spatula through the egg mixture with one hand, and put bread in the toaster with the other. Then he looked at her.

"You're pregnant. Congratulations." The muscles in his jaw stayed rigid.

Ruby's hand fluttered to her throat. "I couldn't tell you until I'd told my aunt and uncle last night." Her voice faltered. "I hadn't even told Mom yet."

"I understand." He asked nothing more, just waited, his charcoal irises pinning her.

Should she tell him everything, expose more of herself than she had already so he'd really know what this meant?

"I was with Ben briefly and we realized we didn't want the same things."

He shook his head, eyes darkening. "A father walked away from his child? How could a man do that?"

The origin of the shadow across his features was obvious. He'd had lymphoma as a teenager and the chemotherapy had made him infertile. The thought of a man abandoning his child would be incomprehensible. She remembered Stella's anguish at the news, but her joy when her son was given the all clear from cancer. Ruby's heart went out to him as it had back then, trying for a second to imagine the enormity, the power, and the finality of such news.

She lifted her face. "Ben never knew I was pregnant. When I called to tell him, I was told he'd been killed in a car accident."

"I'm sorry," he said quietly.

She fixed her gaze on an imperfection on the granite bench top. "So am I. We wouldn't have stayed together, but I'd never deny my baby its father." Ruby ground her fingers into the aching spot at her back as Christo took the pan off the heat. Then he moved around the side of the counter.

"Let me take a look at that back. Hormones often cause tendons to loosen in pregnancy and you can experience some pain."

She sucked in a breath, the alpine clean smell of him invading her in waves as he moved closer. "How do you know about muscles and pregnancy?"

He was within a foot of her, his slightly smiling mouth the only thing she could concentrate on. Why was he looking at her like that, as if she were a flower that needed rearranging, the star that needed straightening on the Christmas tree? He was unwrapping her, looking past her, and seeing right inside to where her heart beat out of time.

Siphoning in a breath, she struggled to stay still, but the next five minutes flashed through her mind. Christo was going to touch her. With his practiced hands he was going to unlock her memories of his body, and she didn't know if she could trust what her own body would do in response.

4

Christo moved closer, his demeanor as calm as when she first stepped in the room. He seemed unconcerned by the announcement of her pregnancy, disinterested even—as if it changed nothing between them.

"When I left college I opened an exclusive private gym with trainers, physiotherapists, and masseurs. I'd worked in gyms to pay my way through my degree, so I knew what I wanted." His deep and husky voice was directly behind her, and fine hairs across the back of her neck rose. "It took me three years to build businesses across the country. Then I put the gyms in exclusive resorts, bought the resorts, and then started to buy the land around them. It all started with a gym."

He'd worked his way up? She fought to hide her surprise. "Did you have backing?"

Lead-bound sincerity laced his words. "Hard work's what got me where I am, Ruby. That and the first-hand experience of having my health compromised. Assisting people to stay in optimal health is important."

His voice was closer now, and Ruby's breath caught

heavily in her throat and she searched for a distraction. "Won't the toast be ready?"

Carefully, he lifted the hair that trailed over her back and laid it over her shoulder, his hand resting on the light fabric of her sweater for an exquisite second. "This won't take a minute."

Instantly, the muscles in her spine were rock hard. Anticipation of him touching her again filled every blood vessel, every cell. Words of refusal clotted in her throat and the air around her sparked.

Was he trying to unhinge her? Perhaps he could see the awakening that beat in her body each time he drew nearer. Maybe now he knew the stakes, he was pulling out his trump card—the knowledge that he could cause her to lose all sense with his touch.

Her mind commanded her lips to move in protest, but her body rebelled. *Just one more time.* Feeling his hands on her skin once more might rid her of the intoxicating memory the years hadn't erased.

The moment he laid his hand on her shoulder it was as if she could lift off the chair. None of her concerns about what he could do to her counted as he began to tease her muscles, manipulate her body. She wanted him to say something, break the spell he'd cast when his skin connected to hers again, but all rational thought had fled. In the silence of the kitchen his fingers probed and smoothed, sending waves of warmth throughout her brittle body.

"Do you mind?" His voice was rich as he lifted the sweater from her back so her thin camisole beneath was exposed, and the vision of him doing that once before floated through her mind. "I'll be able to get at the muscle better without so much distance."

Unable to move or answer, Ruby let him peel the sweater

from her arms, and, as she sat vulnerable on the stool, having the solid presence of him so near, his skin within touching distance caused her heartbeat to spike.

Along the hills and valleys of her spine, his fingers worked their magic, releasing tension from not only the muscles at the surface, but a secret part deep within her.

Did he know what he was doing to her? Could he feel the vibrations from her body teasing his fingers? Maybe he *was* doing this to drive her wild.

"The toast..." Her words came out in a rasping whisper.

Still his fingers probed her back, so Ruby tilted her head and forced insistence into her voice. If he didn't stop now... "Thank you, Christo."

He removed his hands and her skin instantly chilled. "Steven will come this afternoon." He spoke lazily, as if what he'd done was the most natural thing in the world. It probably was, getting what he wanted through charm and seduction. "He'll show you some preventative measures as well. It's important your body's supple and relaxed for the baby."

He stepped away and although relief seeped into her mind, the desire to have him touching her again pulsed deep.

"Thank you." She flexed her shoulder, numb with the warmth and pressure of his hands. "It feels good." She sat straighter in the chair, dragging her sweater back on and trying to bring her heartbeat under control. "You can see how being pregnant changes things for me," she managed. "I want to bring my baby up in the house that's been in my family for generations. I want us to pick apples from the orchard together as I did with my grandmother. Scratch my child's height on the old stable door as my mom did for me." She placed a protective hand on her belly. "I'm sorry, but that's why I can't let you have this house."

He moved around the side of the counter and pulled two plates from a cupboard. "It doesn't change anything. Your generational home hasn't been important to you for the last decade. I can buy you and your baby a much more suitable house. Modern and warm, without a swimming pool and child hazards. I'd say you having a baby's a very good reason for not staying alone in this house."

Even as her body still throbbed with the remains of his touch, disbelief at what he was saying took over. "So my being pregnant doesn't change things for you? It changes things for me. If you'd asked me a few months ago, I never would've dreamed I'd feel so strongly about a place. But now...with my parents gone and this life growing inside me I want to feel connected to my home again. It's important to me, Christo."

He placed the toast on the plates and spooned out eggs. "As I said, I think your pregnancy gives us more options."

She nibbled the inside of her cheek and took her time before answering. "And if we still don't reach an agreement?"

He nodded slowly, his gaze snaring her once more. "We'll reach an agreement."

The final remnants of pleasure her body had held were gone in an instant as her blood chilled.

He passed her the plate and a knife and fork. Her appetite had vanished.

"You won't want this situation dragged on any longer, either," he said, loading the deep yellow eggs onto his fork. "Settling well before the baby's birth is important. Indecision and uncertainty won't help anyone." She watched, mesmerized, as the fork slid into his mouth.

Steadying her own fork, she paused until he'd turned back to face her, a conversation from last night suddenly occurring to her again. "The party on Friday night. We'll need to come to an agreement today so you can go."

"If we need a few more days to negotiate then you'll come with me to the ball."

Her fork wobbled. Being on public display as Christo's date was not what she needed right now. "What makes you think I'd do that?"

He shrugged and then tossed her a powerful smile. "I accompanied you last night. The least you could do is offer me the same consideration."

So he had it all planned. Knew how he could keep her trapped. She couldn't wait to get to the lawyer's office to find a way to end this nightmare.

Sun strike from the harbor beyond the lawyer's window singed Christo's eyes, and he twisted in his seat to focus better on the conversation beside him. This discussion was going nowhere fast and it was time he put an end to it.

"There is no more money," Tim, the lawyer, was saying to Ruby. "Your father had been living beyond his means for years before he died—making sure your mother had no access to his money—and left huge debts. I assume you received nothing when he died."

Ruby's gaze swung to Christo and the burst of pain across her face caused his chest to tighten. "No," she said. "I assumed he left everything to Mom and that when she died the entire estate would be left to me."

"Your mother wasn't negligent in her duty of care toward you," Tim said, "because she's given you a significant share of what she had left. The house."

"But where did the money go?" Ruby asked, her slim

fingers clasped across the desk. "Mom must have had money to maintain the house and pay her housekeeper." She shook her head. "And a whole new wing's been added to the house. Where did *that* money come from?"

Christo shifted in his seat as Tim shuffled some papers. Antonia hadn't had money to pay his mother or maintain the house in years, but he'd been the only other person who knew. And he'd been the one who'd rectified it. They needed to move away from *that* line of questioning as quickly as possible.

"I guess we'll never find out," the lawyer said. "What we do know is that you have a claim to half of the house, as does Mr. Mantazis."

"I can't believe she did this. It seems so...impossible." She perched on the edge of the office chair, a loose dress in deep pink tones flowing across her hips and showcasing toned calf muscles. Her hair that had swung wild and free last night was held tight in a vicious twist, and the prospect of tilting that head back and releasing more than just her hair flared through Christo's veins. His hands still held the memory of her milky skin beneath his touch this morning, and the rest of him burned for the privilege.

"We can move to mediation if you wish." Tim moved from where he'd been pacing in front of the window and sat back in his seat. He seemed to be hitting the main point now, so Christo waited. "Your mother has left Christo half of the house, and unless you can come to some sort of agreement there's going to be a stalemate. And if you're suggesting that there was something untoward in the writing of your mother's will, some sort of duress..."

Ruby held a hand to her face and began twisting a delicate gold ring on her finger. Probably one of her own stylish creations. God, she was beautiful. To think that she was going to be a mother in a few short months. How fortunate she was. Lately Christo had found himself pondering what he'd miss out on, not being a father. For so many years he'd brushed it aside, tried to convince himself being childless didn't matter, but more and more he felt the loss as a physical pain.

"No, no, I'm not suggesting there's anything untoward," Ruby was saying. "It's just such a surprise that I have to share the house, and there's no money to help buy the other half even if Christo agrees." Her brow furrowed deep, and she drew her tongue across her top lip, causing a bullet of desire to shoot through Christo's center. If he were just doing this for sport he'd be happy enough to sit here all day watching her intoxicating face—the way she nibbled her lip as she shifted on the office chair—but this wasn't about him and it was time their little game was over. If Tim didn't suggest a new offer now, then he would.

Ruby's voice strengthened. "But what about my child? Doesn't the fact I'm having a baby make a difference to either of you?" A new fire flared across her face. He noticed it whenever she talked about her baby, and as her chin tilted up that heat seemed to transfer itself to his body. He couldn't prevent a new image looping through his head, of having that fire, that intensity, turned on him in a moment of passion. Moving in his seat, he focused more squarely on the conversation.

Tim looked grave. "I appreciate this is a difficult time for you, Ms. Fleming, but the fact is your mother wasn't aware of any other beneficiaries."

Christo cleared his throat. "Appropriate recompense for your share of the house can still be negotiated."

While Ruby's gaze swung skyward, Tim stood. His tone was hushed as if finally he was on her side, and he turned pointedly toward Christo. "Yes, perhaps you need to consider compensating Ms. Fleming more fully for what she would be losing in this arrangement, Mr. Mantazis. The house is, after all, an historic building on the town's golden mile, which has never been to market. You certainly can't expect her to give it away to you. Given there is no other financial endowment from her mother's estate, she'll find it difficult to support herself and a baby in the interim..."

Ruby twisted her body toward Tim, a frown marring her forehead. Christo slipped a hand in his pocket, then made his move. Reaching across the space separating them, he handed her a check, this time with nothing on it but the signature he'd scrawled in the corner this morning. "You're right, of course, Tim. Pick a number, Ruby, anything you like, and then double it. Bank the check today and you can leave as soon as you're ready. Add on enough to support yourself and your child as long as you need to. It's the best outcome."

Ruby's azure eyes transformed to perfect orbs and then they radiated fury. "You want to buy me, Christo?" Her voice was frozen steel. "You think you can *buy* my future, my baby's birthright, and dictate the end of my family's history in that house? My great-great-grandfather built that house with logs he'd hauled from the forest." Her fingers knotted together in her lap. "He started Fleming Press from the front room and— " Her eyelashes fluttered. "You've no idea, Christo, *no* idea what the best outcome for me and my child is."

She cut the air with her outstretched arm as she brushed the piece of paper away, a double strand of tiny pink pearls around her wrists chattering with the movement.

Christo flicked his gaze to Tim and the lawyer stepped forward. "I feel it would be best if I gave you a moment alone. Without my presence you might be able to gain a little more clarity." He sifted through a pile of papers on his desk and handed her a small white envelope. "Your mother asked that this be given to you on her death. I briefly discussed its contents with her when we last spoke and she assured me it would have no bearing on the will itself. However, it might help with some perspective."

She flung a fiery look at Tim's back as he headed for the door, and she clutched the envelope tight.

Christo wasn't expecting any surprises in the envelope. Antonia had mentioned that she wanted to explain some things she couldn't tell Ruby to her face, but it would be best to divert her attention away from it for now. They had a far more important issue to tackle. "You need to make a decision, Ruby."

When it was just the two of them in the palatial office, she stood and faced him, her face pale under her olive skin. "I want this to stop, Christo. I want this bickering and backward and forward to stop. I want to live in my home with my baby, with your mother if she wants to be there too. I don't know how I'll manage, but I will. I'll find a way to pay you for your half."

The anguished set of her body caused him to lean closer in his seat until he could smell fresh flowers and a cool summer's evening on her skin. An image of her in that house, with her baby—with him—burned itself behind his eyes. "I don't want to hurt anyone," he said calmly, despite the strange mix of confusion and concern cycling through him. "That's not what this is about."

He watched as her eyelids slowly lowered, and he curled his fingers into private fists to prevent himself from reaching out.

And then a solution came to him. A solution so simple

and so sublime he had to think it through again to make sure he hadn't missed anything. The perfection of it caused a smile to pull his mouth before he could stop it. He rose from his chair.

Slowly her eyes drifted open and the glossy blue of their depths pulled him in, made him move to close the gap between them further.

"Marry me."

Her sharp intake of breath cut the air.

"*Marry* you?" She spoke the words slowly, and all he could concentrate on was the swell of her lips as she said them.

He stepped an inch closer, and she tilted her head to look up at him. Her lips parted a fraction, and her breath came whisper soft from her mouth.

"Marry me, and I'll be a father to your baby. My mother will live with us in the house as a real grandmother, and none of you will *ever* want for anything. It's the right solution."

Her body trembled. "You can't be serious, Christo."

A beating heat powered through him at the possibility of what he could create for his mother and for the child growing inside Ruby. A life he could share with Ruby. His pulse spiked. The certainty that this would work to abject perfection pumped through his body.

"I've never been more serious. Marry me, Ruby, and all of our problems will be over."

5

"There is no alternative." Christo stood facing her on the pavement below the lawyer's office, cars and buses racing past in the sultry afternoon heat. Despite the fantastical nature of his words, his face radiated a singular confidence. "Your mother didn't offer a solution if we couldn't agree. If you won't sell the house to me then we'll share it. A marriage will both serve as a contract on the ownership of the house and as security for your child's future."

Marriage? To *Christo?* The world tilted beneath her feet.

Once it had been all she'd dreamed of, before those dreams had been shattered into a million pieces. Now all she was left with was stark reality.

Swallowing hard, she turned her face to his, the sun's reflection on the window of a building behind him searing her vision. Why would he propose something so outrageous? A marriage without love. She didn't know about him, but for her, that was completely impossible.

"You'd marry me just so your mother can stay on in the house?"

He raised the aviator glasses to his face then stopped, nodding slowly. "My mother wouldn't live there if she didn't think she was entitled, so yes, for my mother." He leaned fractionally closer, his stare trapping her. "Your baby would have a father. You'd both be supported financially. Stay in the house as my wife, and in years to come it'll pass to your child as you want. I'd see to that."

The sincerity in the lines deepening on his face stayed with her as she swiveled and began to walk to somewhere there was more air, where she could think—just somewhere away from Christo's heated gaze, and from the impossible solution he'd proposed.

His footfalls equaled hers as they headed toward the waterfront and the harbor sparkling in the distance like a jeweled blanket. The spirit of this place that had begun as a tug when she'd arrived now hauled her in cell-by-cell, and she couldn't ignore it. She belonged here. So did her baby. In this town. In that house. Her *home*.

But not with Christo living there. A home should be a place full of love, a haven to relax and let your guard down —things she could never do with Christo in the same house.

"A marriage for how long?" she wondered aloud. "Until your mother is settled and you can move me and my baby out?"

His voice was a low rumble beside her, dark but sure. "A marriage forever. I'm Greek Orthodox, Ruby. The lifelong commitment of marriage is important in my culture. I don't make a contract then back out of it."

A marriage contract. To be drawn up as a way to break this impasse. How could he have even thought it possible, let alone said it aloud?

Each revelation in the past twelve hours had been a shock, but this was a king-hit delivered direct to her chest, and once again her brain scrambled for a way out. Maybe the letter Tim had given her would hint at a solution? But she'd need to be alone to read something as personal as her mother's final words to her.

Just ahead, a woman swerved a stroller toward them to avoid a workman in a manhole and Christo dragged her close. She sucked in a breath as a shroud of protective heat enveloped her body and, slightly dizzy, she tried to right herself only to be assailed by an intense awareness of the man holding her. Memories of needing Christo's touch in the past couldn't match her desire for him now. Every nerve ending cried out for that strong, certain caress that was branded in her body's memory.

With her elbow cradled in his palm, Christo guided her into the veranda of a restaurant as a stream of people funneled past. She stepped back into the shadow of a black-and-white-striped awning, heart tripping, body sparking.

She blinked, trying to focus on why they were here, to negotiate a solution for the house.

She swallowed. "Your mother wouldn't want you to have a sham marriage for the sake of a house. I know she wouldn't."

"My mother would believe it was a traditional, committed marriage or she wouldn't stay. You know how important her faith is to her."

Ruby couldn't believe she was standing here, calmly discussing the details of his proposal as if it was a rational suggestion. As if it were possible. That he could speak of a marriage in such a calculated and cool tone caused her heart to chill.

"Your offer's generous, Christo. I appreciate that you're trying to propose a solution, but I'll find a way out of this. And I'll find a way to support my baby."

He swung around so his back was turned to the push of pedestrians, and his gaze locked on her. "My offer is on the table for two days."

Swallowing, she backed closer to the wall behind her. "Two days? Why?"

Slowly, he took a step nearer, and the sun was blocked completely, his broad chest a touch away, his breath warm on her cheek. Mouth set in a straight line, his eyes shone. "I don't expect you to agree today, but when you think this through, get over the shock, you'll see it's the right decision. The only one. Neither of us will let the other have the house. Marriage so your baby's inheritance is assured is the logical solution."

She pulled in air, drugged by the certainty on his face. *Could* it be possible? "But why a time limit?"

"I'm offering you a new kind of family, Ruby. A father for your baby, and a grandmother who will love your child as if it were her own. But I won't wait endlessly for your answer."

Mouth beginning to dry, she stroked the skin at her throat, trying to ease her breathing. *Family*. He couldn't know the power of that word, how she ached because her child would never know its family. "Those things would benefit me and my baby, Christo, but why would you turn your life upside down like that? What on Earth would you gain apart from the house? *Another* possession?"

A muscle at his jaw pulsed for the merest second. "A son. A daughter."

His hand braced the brick lintel above her head, and when he leaned in a swell of understanding gripped her. A child he could call his own. The grandchild he thought he couldn't give his mother. Everything had changed since yesterday. Now it was about so much more than his quest to gain the house from her. Now he wanted her to provide a son or daughter too. She'd once dreamed of them being parents together, growing their love in a family, but the thought of him asking her to do this so dispassionately sent icy fingers across her skin.

"But your mother would know this baby wasn't yours," she rasped.

"Of course she'll know the biological truth, but the child will be mine in everything but genetics."

Reality punched her in the chest. As he'd always done, Christo would use her for what she could provide—the things that lay outside his grasp. He didn't need her for status or money this time; now he needed her for the house he couldn't secure for his mother, for the baby he would never father, and for the grandchild he desperately wanted to produce. He was an only child, the son his mother's life had orbited since she'd brought him here from Greece as a baby. With all the sacrifices she'd made for him and his resulting successes, it was so achingly clear why he wanted to give her a grandchild.

Being around someone who knew exactly what he wanted, someone who was passionate enough to toss everything aside to win it, was intoxicating. It had taken her breath away about him in the past. Yet he'd use her to acquire these things in the same way he'd used her before.

He dropped his voice. "You won't regret sharing the house with me." He lifted a hand as if to touch her, graze his thumb down her cheek, but then stopped. "It's time we acknowledged our past and moved beyond it, Ruby. We both know what each other is capable of and why a relationship between us was doomed. Now we can come to an arrangement to suit us both. Given there's no money from the estate, have you thought about how you'll support your baby?"

She lifted her chin and met his stare. "I'll find work here. I still have some publishing contacts."

"You'd have to work full time, earn a decent living to maintain that enormous old house and grounds. That means your baby would be in full-time care."

She rolled her lip between her teeth. With all the revelations in the past few days, everything had changed. She'd planned as far ahead as coming home and telling her mother she was pregnant, praying for a reconciliation, and then beginning a whole new chapter in her life. But now that her mother was gone, now that she'd have to maintain the house on her own with a baby, admittedly it did feel...scary. But she'd find a way to make it work.

"With my offer, and my mother at home to child-mind, you could work part time, full time, whatever you pleased, knowing your baby was being cared for by family. Or I could support you fully so you could spend all day together. You know it's the right decision, Ruby." He paused, and all she could focus on was the set of his lips as he'd said her name, and she wanted him to say it again. His grin was slow. "Two days. You'll agree by then."

She shook her head as she tried to expel her body's reaction to him, but she met the full threat of his gaze. "And when I say no?"

His chin tilted, and she noticed the change from smooth skin this morning to swarthy stubble now. How would that rugged skin feel against her cheek? Imagining the sweet pleasure-pain as his skin grazed hers sent spikes of warmth through her. The fantasy swelled in her mind until she caught his intense look and wondered if he felt it too.

He shrugged one jacketed shoulder and the corner of his mouth lifted more. "For two days we get to know each other again, work out the practicalities. I guarantee by then you'll see the benefits of becoming my wife."

There it was—in that instant she could feel herself slipping under Christo's spell again. It wouldn't happen this time, though, not when her baby depended on her to make the right choices. She moved as if to slide away from the seductive hold he had over her. "If you don't mind, I'd like some privacy to read through my mom's letter."

He raised a dark eyebrow. "You want me to go back to the house alone? An opportunity for me to call Tim back and say you've run off again. As you did ten years ago."

The mention of the way she'd left before stung, but she held his sparking stare. "It wasn't like that last time. It wasn't me who ran off."

The throng behind them had thinned, but still he stayed close, his voice dropping to a deep hum. "What happened last time, Ruby? You left and hardly ever came back. Your plan to use me to shock your father had obviously worked, so why leave when you finally had his full attention? Or was that all part of the game?"

She looked left and right, then let her gaze drift back to his face. "I'm not talking about it here, on the pavement."

He touched her elbow again and spoke low, nodding at the bar behind them. "Let's go in here. You can read your mother's letter while I get us a drink."

She paused and then nodded before he ushered her through the door.

Minutes later she sat at a table by the corner of the bar, wondering at her decision to step inside this place. Slow fans moved the sticky air overhead, and she pulled off the linen jacket glued to her back. Twisting her fingers around the leather strap on her bag, she watched Christo at the bar, standing as if he owned the place. God, considering all she'd learned in the last two days, he probably did.

With a trembling finger, she lifted the flap on the envelope and withdrew a small piece of flowered notepaper.

Dearest Ruby,

I should have explained this long ago, but with the way things were between us I wanted my words written down, not lost in some tense conversation. I know things must feel very confusing to you right now, so I'd like to try and help you understand.

Heartbeat stuttering, eyes filling with tears, Ruby read on.

I've left the house to both you and Christo for two reasons. The first is that I have no money to offer you, and Christo has promised he'll pay a very generous amount for your share.

Of course I know how you feel about him, and I suspect if I hadn't made him a beneficiary you would've refused to sell to him. But I want him to have the house, Ruby. I've known for a long time that the scars caused by my relationship with your father have cut so deep you'll never return here for good, so it's my last wish that Christo buys the house for Stella, my most loyal and dearly loved friend, who deserves to spend the rest of her days in what has, for so long, been her home.

There is much I wish I'd told you about what happened between me and your father, but I'm not sure it's what you'd want to hear right now. Christo knows the whole story, should you be interested one day. But in the meantime I wish you every happiness and success in your life in New York, my darling. I hope the money you receive from Christo will allow you to live the dreams you've so bravely chosen to follow.

All my love forever,

Mom

Heart racing, Ruby flicked the page over, desperate for

something more. No explanation for her affair? No acknowledgement of the pain they'd all been through? Disappointment and a slow, gnawing sadness dragged through her.

Her mother wanted Christo to have the house. She wanted Stella to live there. It was no longer just an assertion from Christo. The truth was here in black and white. Tears burned the back of her nose and, too tired, too heartsick to hold them back, she let one fall.

"Sparkling orange?"

Quickly wiping her eyes as Christo put a glass and bottle down, she tried to still the whirl of confusion in her head.

"I wasn't sure what was appropriate when pregnant, whether soda was okay or if there was too much sugar."

Her fingers moved across her belly. If only she'd had a chance to see her mother again, tell her about the pregnancy and that she'd put their past behind them. Maybe they could've lived in the house and brought up her baby together.

Christo unscrewed the cap, poured the foaming liquid into a glass, and handed it to Ruby. She'd caught a lip between her teeth and nibbled it in that sweet way of hers. "It says it's organic," he said, pulling the conversation back to safer ground. "Which reminds me, I made a call to Alec, one of my restaurant managers, and he'll be sourcing the best produce for a daily delivery to the house. I didn't ask you this morning if you're suffering from morning sickness."

Ruby pinched the bridge of her nose and closed her eyes. When her lids fluttered open, the sadness cut straight through him.

He leaned forward. "Is everything all right?" He nodded

at the piece of paper still clutched in her hand. "Did it help?"

"Help?" she whispered.

"Convince you?"

She laced her fingers together and stared at her drink. "I was hoping it would give me a way out," she said with a sigh. "Something I could take back to Tim or my lawyer, but it's the opposite. The whole letter explains why she left the house to both of us and why she wants you to buy me out." She paused as her voice shook. "If Mom felt so strongly about you and Stella having the house, then maybe it's time I honored her wishes and gave it up."

Christo put his palm flat on the table. She couldn't back out now. Things had changed too much, morphed into possibilities he never could have imagined in the beginning. "But she didn't know about your baby."

"No, she didn't." She touched the tiny pink beads of her pearl bracelet, moving each one like a rosary.

"She may have changed her will if she had."

She wiped her hand across her cheek as if brushing away tears. "Maybe you're right. Mom mightn't have done the right thing for her immediate family, but she was so close to her brothers Lorenzo and Matteo that I'm sure she would have been different as a grandmother."

He rolled a shoulder as the tension inside him eased. "Is that why you stayed away? Because your relationship with your mother had broken down?"

For a second it seemed as if she'd deflect his question. He willed her to give him an answer, to confirm his suspicion that she'd been avoiding him all these years.

Brushing a blonde strand over her shoulder, she shifted in her chair. "I didn't want to be here anymore."

He lifted a bottle of beer to his lips but spoke before he

drank. "And you didn't want to come back and see your mother? Your father before he died?"

She pulled the lip between her teeth again. Damn if he'd let himself be distracted.

"I was in touch with my father. I came for the occasional holiday."

"That's all?"

She leaned forward and her voice dropped. "I found out some things that changed the way I viewed my parents, my family."

He rested his wrists on the table and clasped his hands together. Should he feign innocence, or finally reveal the truth, the things she didn't know about her family? "Things?"

"I found out..." She hesitated and moistened her lips. "That my mother had been having an affair."

He nodded slowly, keeping his features neutral. "I see."

She took another sip of the soda. "Not just a one night stand or a fling. My mother had been having an affair for years."

"How did you find out?"

"I heard her on the phone one night," she said softly, "not long after you'd been sent away, and I questioned her."

The memory of how he'd felt the evening he was banished was still so vivid, but he pushed it aside. "And how was she?"

"She didn't deny it. Said she was sorry I'd had to find out like that." Leaning back, she crossed her arms under her breasts, the pain of telling him stamped on her face. "And then I knew I couldn't live under the same roof while she did that to my father. I couldn't see him devastated, so I told her I'd keep her little secret, and I left. It was the best thing for everyone."

He dragged a hand through his hair. "And you never spoke to her about it again?"

She shook her head. "I don't know what happened to her lover. I never even found out who he was or how long the affair continued. My parents stayed in the house together until my father died of a stroke, so she was either still keeping things a secret, or she'd moved on. We pretended it wasn't there in the beginning, that in not discussing it, it wasn't real." She drew in a long and labored breath. "But the less we talked, the more distant we became."

He dropped an arm to the table and scraped his other hand across his chin, all the while holding her gaze to his. It was now or never, let her know everything or shut this conversation down.

The air between them stilled and he heard the breath draining from Ruby's lungs. "What do you know, Christo? Mum said in the letter that if I wanted to know more to ask you."

Tilting his head, he shrugged. "There's no need to go over all this, Ruby."

"Need? Of course there's a need. In the space of two days I've found out the ownership of my childhood home is in dispute, that there's no money to fight it, and I have to marry to get what's rightfully mine. In seven months I'll have a child who's lost most of its family, a child who deserves to have me fight for any link to its heritage, including that house." She blew out a breath. "Yes, there *is* a need."

Christo hesitated then frowned, weighing up how much to tell her. The power and passion in her voice caused him to hesitate. "It won't change anything."

"I need to understand. Maybe if I understand what's led us here I can find a way out."

He leaned back in his chair, surveying her, and the desperation in her soft face unbuckled a part of him that had been locked down for years. "Your father knew about your mother's affair. He was blackmailing her by threatening that if she didn't stay with him he'd publish an expose on her brother's crooked business dealings, Lorenzo's links to gambling dens, and corporate embezzlement."

Ruby fell against the back of the chair as if his words had been a physical force. Her voice dipped. "Mom stayed with him to protect Uncle Lorenzo?"

"And to protect you."

She watched him warily. "How would that protect me?"

"Are you sure you want to know this? After all this time?"

She looked at him without flinching. "Tell me everything, Christo. I need to know."

He nodded once, satisfied she was ready. "He said you'd never be able to work in publishing back here if your uncle was exposed. Your mother was desperate for you to come back and would have done anything to make it happen. Your father knew that if the scandal came out, not only would he have no chance at the local government career he wanted, you'd have no future in Brentwood Bay either."

She shook her head. "Why didn't my mom tell me any of this? My father's been dead for over a year. Surely she could have told the truth after that."

Christo shrugged. "She knew you idolized him. And since she believed everything was lost between you, she thought it was better for this to be left unsaid."

Ruby stared at a watermark on the table where her bottle had sat. "I don't know whether to feel more sorry for Mom, or Dad. To go to those sorts of lengths, Dad must've been desperate to stay with her."

Christo scoffed. "Desperate to keep his own public

persona squeaky clean." The injustice of being banished seared hot in his memory. "Your father had a procession of girlfriends. The night before he kicked me out, he'd seen me at a society polo match. I saw him with a couple of much younger women. That was the real reason he threw me out. He didn't want you to know."

~

Ruby fought the nausea climbing in her throat. She didn't want to revisit that night right now or listen to Christo's excuses. The news about her father blackmailing her mother was enough to cope with. "Did my mother have a procession of lovers as well?"

Christo shook his head. "Just one. For fifteen years."

"Fifteen?" An ache of confusion burned behind Ruby's eyes. "Does that mean...she was still with him when she died?"

He nodded slowly, and she scoured her mind as to who it might've been. "One of her friends? Someone I knew?"

"Someone you knew very well. Someone who lost his home about the same time I did."

Ruby's heart stopped beating. "David? The gardener, David?" She remembered the quiet man with the gentle smile. As a little girl she'd taken his hand as they'd walked the flowerbeds, and he'd recited the names of the roses her mother had loved so much. She'd helped him bring bunches of them to fill the house with vibrant color, sweet perfume. Things her mother had held so dear.

"He was the love of her life. He left for Europe when your mother died."

Like a wave building from the depths of the ocean floor,

Ruby realized what had happened all those years ago and tears began to sting.

Christo spoke her thoughts. "Your father didn't want the shame of your mother having an affair with the hired help. He didn't want that from you either. Both revelations would've tainted his shiny public image."

Ruby slumped back in her chair as Christo's announcements spun a web around her. "Did he care about it that much?"

"He was standing for council. His reputation as a big shot publisher should've stood him in good stead. If the fact that both his wife and daughter had been having affairs with the hired help got out, it might've affected voters. As would a scandal where his wife left him for the gardener."

Ruby sat in stunned silence for what seemed like an eternity. Christo waited, sipping his drink, giving her the time she needed to gather together all the scattered pieces. One thought pushed above all the others.

"You knew all this when he kicked you out and you didn't tell me?" It was a betrayal—keeping information about her own family from her, as if he knew what was best.

Christo gave a cold laugh. "You didn't want to know the truth, Ruby. About me or your mother."

She couldn't help bitterness slipping into her voice. "You're saying you weren't dating other women? That being at that polo match was for the enjoyment of the game and nothing more? I asked you for an explanation back then, but you couldn't get away quickly enough."

For a moment, his mask dropped and he looked at her with frank honesty. "I was nineteen, Ruby. Cancer free and ready to meet the world head on. A boy who could suddenly see the full implications of the difference between the haves and have-nots. Before you and I became close, I had offers and propositions, women who said they could take me places. I won't deny being at that polo match to develop connections for my business ideas, but I wasn't dating anyone else. As we began spending time together, you were all I could think about."

A flush swept her body. Was he speaking the truth?

It didn't matter. His charm was part of what had made her fall so heavily for him before. The fact that he could use it to suit any need, or any person—honorable or not—was what made him so untrustworthy. Whether he'd cheated on her or not, he was using her for his own gain back then and he was still doing it now. "All I knew from that time is that you didn't want to communicate with me after my father told you to leave. I waited for an explanation, but you gave me nothing. Instead of finding me and answering my questions, you left and never returned. I didn't serve your purpose anymore."

"And I didn't serve yours. You'd shocked your father by beginning a relationship with me, as was your plan all along. If you'd had faith in me you wouldn't have needed an explanation."

"Faith is earned through identifiable actions, Christo. Respecting someone enough to move heaven and earth to give them the answers they deserve. Not using people for your own ends." Pushing their history to the side to think about later, she refocused on her family. "I don't understand why Mom stayed with Dad, though. If he was so awful, why did she remain in the house?"

"She had no choice. She'd poured all her own money into rescuing Lorenzo. Your father had control of the house. David had lost his home and his job. Your mother was trapped through blackmail."

A vision of her mother, trapped and lonely, filled her

mind. She twisted in her seat, body aching with the tension in her limbs. "At least she had the house when he died."

He shook his head. "She didn't even have that. Your father had it tangled up in a complicated trust. Only after she fought through the courts when he died were the house and grounds returned to her name."

"If things were that tight, how on Earth did she afford things like the upkeep and your mother's wages?"

"I paid for everything."

Ruby gasped, but after all she'd discovered in the last day she shouldn't have been surprised. "Mom was such a proud person. I can't imagine her accepting your money."

His shoulder lifted in a lazy shrug. "She didn't know it was mine. I arranged it with her lawyer. As far as she knew the cash came from some bonds your father had forgotten to hide from her."

Her heart swelled for what he'd done for his mother and hers. "That was an incredibly generous thing to do."

"If I hadn't, the house would've fallen into disrepair and my mother would've lost the job she held dear, the home she loved."

As his declaration sank in, Ruby tried to untangle the ruthless, take-no-prisoners Christo from the man who'd sheltered her mother from more heartbreak. How could she dig beneath his steely exterior to find the softer part of his heart that must beat sometimes?

"What I don't understand is why Mom did the same thing my father did in his will. Instead of passing the house on to their next of kin, both left it in tangled and complicated circumstances where their family has to fight for it."

"Understand this." His voice had returned to the distant, cold tone she'd heard so often in the last two days. "My mother stood by Antonia through your father's recriminations and double life, through you abandoning her, through Lorenzo's shady deals. Antonia wanted to acknowledge my mother, but she wanted to provide for you too. She couldn't leave the house to my mother outright, so she left it to both you and me, knowing I had the wherewithal to buy you out. That way both of you would be taken care of. She hadn't counted on any resistance from you."

"If only I'd known all this, she and I could've talked about it, sorted things out. If she'd only given me the chance." Her heart squeezed. "But now it's too late."

"It's not too late for your baby. One decision can change everything."

Her head spun as she watched him warily. He could so easily push his advantage now if he wanted to—remind her what the letter had said about her mother wanting Stella to have it. But this wasn't just about the house anymore. Now he wanted so much more from her. He wanted her child.

"So, how do you know all this?" she asked. "Why would Mom have opened up to you about it?"

He leaned closer, both hands together only inches from hers. The light from the wall behind him cast shadows across his face, making him look not so very different from the nineteen-year-old boy she'd fallen in love with a lifetime ago. "Your mother welcomed me back in the house after your father died, and we became closer. She understood that, like her, I'd been maligned and maltreated by your father and by you."

She ignored the barb. "I'm glad you were there for her, Christo."

"And I'll be here for you too. Both you and your baby."

She swallowed. "Even though you now know this was all kept from me, you'll still fight on?"

His unrelenting gaze held her motionless. "Now that *you*

understand everything—why your mother felt so indebted to my mother—you must see now that marriage is the only solution. Antonia wanted my mother to have that house. You want it too."

"What you're offering me wouldn't be a real family. How can I do that to my child?"

He was so close now she could see each one of his inky black lashes. "It would be a lot healthier than the family you had," he said. "This baby will have two parents who would do anything for their child. *Available* parents whose relationship wasn't diseased by unrequited love or unreasonable expectation. I know you, Ruby, and you know me. There will be no surprises, no emotional rollercoasters. We're both strong, passionate people who'll put a child first. Your child can have a live-in grandmother who would love him like her own."

"And parents who don't share a bedroom."

He hooked her with a look of soft desire. "I don't see why not."

She couldn't disguise her shock. "So you'd want the marriage to be consummated?"

"Of course. Our marriage would be for life, so what choice would there be? I'd never break my vows and look outside the union."

Ruby placed both palms flat on the table and stared straight into his eyes as her heart beat out of her chest. "If making love is a requirement of this marriage of convenience then there is absolutely no way I'll agree. *Ever.*"

She'd once loved him with her mind, but that had been when she'd also loved him with her heart. She wouldn't fall into his arms. He was a different man. Older. Cynical. More calculating. And he still only wanted her for what she could provide. There was something hard and cold inside him now. She couldn't let herself forget that.

He arched an eyebrow. "So, you're saying that without sex you'll agree to a marriage? That we'll share the house so our child can grow up in a healthy family? An emotionally stable family?"

Ruby lifted her chin. There were no more options, no other way to right the wrongs of the past, to give her baby the opportunity to grow up in the home of its ancestors. His point that they knew each other so well, strengths and weaknesses, had touched something in her and she wondered if that might, indeed, be the best environment to bring a baby up in.

"If we draw up watertight agreements and contracts to safeguard the house, if we agree to a commitment to my child's future, and if we agree to no sex—then, yes, I'll marry you."

Christo leaned fractionally closer. "Let's start with that," he said.

6

"Ready?" Christo asked as he held the sleek door of his convertible open for Ruby.

Moments earlier they'd glided through enormous security gates, driven down a densely wooded driveway, and pulled up at a grand entrance staircase. It had been almost twenty-four hours since she'd agreed to marry Christo, but it still felt like a dream. A fantasy. And yet it felt strangely possible. Something had shifted deep inside when Christo had told her the truth about her parents, like a part of her that had been buried was beginning to find the light.

"I thought you said your mother was in your *apartment*." She looked up at the enormous dwelling that blocked the afternoon sun. "This is almost as big as my..." She tripped on the words. "It's almost as big as the estate." The modern wooden and steel structure sat magnificently on a plateau overlooking the sparkling waters of Brentwood Bay. With Tantillo Island in the distance, the view was the same as the view from her own front garden, give or take a few degrees on the compass.

"Technically, it's an apartment," he said, as he shut the

car door. "With separate entranceways, but I can make it into a single dwelling if I wish." Guiding her up the stairs, he placed his palm at the small of her back and immediately a shower of sparks raced through her midriff.

A primal craving for more of his touch flared from somewhere within, but she pushed it away and forced herself to listen to him.

"The penthouse suite at the top is where my mother is. The other apartments below are for family who visit from Greece."

"It's beautiful," she whispered.

"Not according to my mother." The pressure of his palm increased as he ushered her through the giant wooden doors, and she had to focus harder on what he was saying. "I bought this a few years ago, hoping to convince her that it would be a great place for her retirement. Sea views and lush gardens as she's used to, a cook's kitchen with a specially planted garden with all her Greek herbs. She wouldn't hear of it. Wouldn't think of leaving your mother."

Her heart warmed. Ruby had always loved Stella, but all this new knowledge, the lengths she'd gone to for Antonia, made her want to thank Christo's mother in person. One good thing to come out of all of this was that she would have Stella Mantazis back in her life—as a grandmother to her child.

Inside, across an expansive marble floor, they reached an elevator and Christo pressed the up-arrow. He slung a hand in the pocket of his pale chinos and looked at her. "I've confirmed to the organizing committee at tomorrow's event that I'll attend and you'll be accompanying me."

Ruby nodded, then tilted her face to his. "So, we're still playing by the rules of leaving the house together?"

His broad shoulders straightened. "I'll inform Tim today

about our plans, but until we're married and the finer print of the contract has been discussed, it's prudent to follow the terms of the will."

Obviously he didn't trust that she'd stick to their agreement. Despite the intensity of yesterday's proposal, he was still doing everything to keep her at arm's length. And did that mean she couldn't leave without his permission?

She clasped her hands together in front and pushed calm into her voice. "Then that could be a problem." He swung his gaze to her as she continued. "Now I've made the commitment to stay in Brentwood Bay, I'll need to return to New York to sell my apartment and make plans for my things to be shipped. I have good friends I want to say goodbye to, but I'll be back within the week."

She'd spent much of the morning making arrangements —handing in her notice at the magazine, putting her apartment on the market. She'd expected to feel apprehensive, that she'd second-guess her decision to stay in Brentwood Bay permanently under these circumstances, but as each tie from her old life was cut, she felt more and more sure she'd made the right decision for her child. And for her. She'd already imagined hunting out her old swing chair to hang back up in the ancient apple tree. And she'd lain awake last night planning which bedroom she could turn into a nursery.

His dark eyes flared. "A return to New York right now's impossible. A marriage license takes at least three days to organize and then there's the venue to arrange, guest lists to draw up. Your trip will need to wait until we're married."

She paused, and her throat dried. "You'd imagined an elaborate occasion? I couldn't go through with this sort of marriage in a church. No, it's not possible."

"Our marriage will demonstrate our commitment to the

agreement. Something that can be witnessed by your family, and my mother especially. I want there to be no doubt in anyone's mind that this is a marriage, a commitment to be honored."

She swallowed. A traditional ceremony certainly wasn't what she'd imagined. She'd pictured just enough to tick the official boxes, ensure the security of the house, and a future for her baby. The thought of standing in a church in a pure white gown put a whole different spin on things. "My trip can't wait, Christo. I owe it to my employer to wrap up my job properly. And I want to ensure I get the best price for my apartment. I need to go as soon as possible."

His tone became cooler. "I won't live in limbo, Ruby." His gaze flicked to the elevator door as if he was done with this conversation. "As I told you from the start, I have commitments, and this situation will be settled so I can see to them. I understand that you need to tie things up in New York, but this impasse won't be truly resolved until we're married." His chin jutted a little higher as the elevator announced its arrival.

Ruby bit back a response for now. This sense of entitlement was not the way he used to behave but was what she'd witnessed since she'd been back. He was obviously used to getting his own way these days, expecting everyone to do what he wanted without compromising himself. He wasn't going to change his mind here, and she wanted to keep things pleasant today for his mother. She'd find a way to postpone the wedding until after she'd returned from New York, or else she'd just leave. He wanted too much from her now to stand in her way.

The elevator doors slid open and Christo gestured that she should enter—no hand on her back this time. She watched his implacable profile in the mirrored doors of the elevator and tried to read his thoughts. For Christo, this marriage to her was simply another entry in his diary, another of his chances to make the most of an opportunity, as any good entrepreneur would. And that's the way she'd view it, too. A contract to secure what she needed for herself and her baby.

The steely set of his shoulders, the uncompromising confidence that always accentuated his features—a small thrill ran through her as she imagined that look on their wedding day. Their wedding night. Yet they'd agreed the wedding night wouldn't be traditional—they'd retire to separate bedrooms.

"Your mother is expecting us, isn't she?" she asked as she flattened her dress with damp palms. "It won't be too much of a shock? The news of the marriage?"

"Shock?" Christo let out a throaty laugh. "News that I'm getting married will eclipse any event this century for my mom. Shock won't come into it. I sent a driver to pick up my Aunt Kiki and take her shopping so we could have a private moment with Mom."

The elevator came to a halt. The doors slid open and Ruby's heart leapt into her mouth.

She'd expected a hallway, a foyer at the very least so she could prepare herself for this reunion, but they'd arrived smack bang in the middle of Christo's living room, and his mother was standing in front of them, arms outstretched, a beaming smile on her face as she'd always had. Suddenly Christo's hand, strong and sure, slid into hers. Her pulse quickened as her mind flew to his hand holding hers on their wedding day. *Any* day after when she'd be sharing his house, his *life*.

"Ruby *mou*!" The older woman enveloped Ruby in a hug, the softly sweet smell of face powder and herbs bringing tears to her eyes. "It is so good to see you, my darling, and I am so, so sorry for the loss of your precious mother." Ruby wanted to fall into the arms of Stella Manatzis and the security her hugs always gave, but all the blood in her body was racing to the place where her hand joined Christo's. Warm and firm, the connection suddenly loosened every bone in her body.

"Thank you so much, Stella, for everything you did for Mom for so long."

"It has been too long, *koukla*." Stella stepped back and gripped the gold cross around her neck. And then her gaze snapped to where Ruby's hand was twined with Christo's, and her mouth dropped open. "You two?" Her sparkling black eyes grew rounder as her voice became more shrill. "You *two*?" In rapid fire Greek she threw up her hands and turned to Christo before taking his face in her hands and kissing him on both cheeks.

"Mama," Christo said when he'd withdrawn from the kiss, "Ruby and I have some news." He laid a hand on Ruby's shoulder and pulled her close until the warm planes of his torso were solid and sure beside her. "We're getting married."

"*A Panagia mou*!" Stella made the sign of the cross three times and her tear-filled eyes swung skyward. "After so many bad times and so much sadness, you have been drawn together by God and by dear Antonia's passing."

Christo smiled and, still holding Ruby close, placed a kiss on each of his mother's cheeks. A memory of a young Christo—a deeply caring son, a passionate friend—touched Ruby, and for a moment she couldn't reconcile the apprehension of becoming his wife with the knowledge that she'd once loved him so much.

"Come in, come in!" Stella bustled toward a table laden

with food. "Ruby-*mou*, Christo said you were coming, so I made some sweets. Sit, sit!" She waved a white handkerchief that she'd dabbed her face with. "You must tell me the whole story," she said turning back to them. "Christo, this is a celebration, we need some cherry brandy for good luck and many years together."

Christo drew Ruby closer once more, and her body seemed imprinted with his strong chest and his protective arms.

"No cherry brandy, Mom." His palm rubbed slow circles at the base of Ruby's spine, sending a shower of delicious tingles through her lower body. "Ruby is pregnant."

His mother's salt and pepper eyebrows moved down, then rapidly up. "Ah-me, it is a miracle!" Stella cried, and again she made the sign of the cross. "And those doctors telling us there was no hope for babies after the cancer." She nodded vigorously. "But I have lit candles at the church and prayed for ten years that they had made a mistake..."

"No, Mama." Christo's voice was low and grave. "The baby's father was from New York. He died before Ruby could tell him. I'll be the father now. And the estate will be your new home. We'll all live there together. The four of us."

Once more, Stella dabbed the handkerchief to her eyes and slumped in an easy chair. "This morning I am an old woman staying in her son's house baking *melomacarona* and wondering what will become of me, and now I will have a daughter-in-law and a baby, too! And I can stay in that blessed house. Christo, my heart is bursting!"

The truth, the sincerity, the absolute love and acceptance in Stella's voice, gripped Ruby's heart and squeezed the air from her lungs. Slowly the room began to swim. A vase of flowers on the table became a brilliant blur as Stella's voice rang in her head. "This baby will have a whole new family in Brentwood Bay," she was saying. "Just as Antonia would want for you, Ruby. When you are Christo's wife, he will be the father of your beautiful *morou*."

Vertigo gripped Ruby and she swayed on her feet. She felt herself buckle, begin to disintegrate before something solid and strong caught her fall and she felt herself floating, lifted above the turmoil in her head to a place of beauty and serenity.

The next moment her eyes were fluttering open and Christo was holding a wet compress to her forehead as she lay on a couch. "Enough excitement for one day. Take some deep breaths. I'm calling a doctor." His voice rumbled low in her ear, his fresh marine scent enough to ease her skipping pulse.

"What happened?" She drew her dry tongue across her lips, trying to focus on his jawline so close.

"The excitement level in this room hit overdrive, and you were affected by it. I told Mom everything at once, but I see you weren't expecting it."

"Stella?" Ruby struggled to look around and sit up, but Christo's warm palm on her shoulder eased her back into the comforting cushions.

"She's gone to the kitchen to heat up egg-lemon soup. It's a great tonic for pregnancy, apparently." He pulled a phone from his pocket, his gaze still trained on her face. There was something there. Anxiety? Concern?

"I don't need a doctor, Christo, I'm fine," she said as her head pounded.

He ignored her protest and punched the keypad, that cast-iron confidence returning once more. "A check-up will do no harm. I can't have you coming out tomorrow night if you're not well."

Letting her eyes close, Ruby concentrated on the cool,

firm pressure of the damp cloth on her forehead and the sense of Christo, so near as he spoke commandingly on the phone. When he'd finished, she opened her eyes.

"We lied to your mother, Christo." Her voice was a whisper.

He placed the phone on the table and leaned close once more. "Lied? We didn't lie." He shrugged a shoulder as his face darkened. "I said we're getting married, you're pregnant, that we'll live in the house together. Facts."

Her mouth was parched, tongue heavy in her mouth. "We lied by omission. Your mother thinks we're in love."

Despite the fizz through her blood each time he touched her, despite the new thrill she'd begun to feel when he spoke of their future, he didn't love her. He saw her as a means to an end, as he always had, only this time he was completely honest about it.

His stare intensified. "You need to give my mother some credit, Ruby. She had an arranged marriage to my father when she was a teenager. She knows that people marry for all sorts of reasons."

"I thought your father treated your mother badly."

He looked to the kitchen, then back again, and his voice dropped low. "He did, which was why she left Greece when she was pregnant with me. She wanted me as far away from him as she could get, so she came to live in Brentwood Bay where her brother Mano was living. She, of all people, would understand that you do what you have to for a baby. Which is precisely what you are doing."

The familiar feeling of being influenced by Christo's confidence, slipping under his spell, began to call to her, but she blocked it. "So why don't you tell her the truth about everything...like the house?"

His jaw was rigid. "Because it would cause her pain. She

must believe she has as much right to live in the house as if it were her own. Not that she's there by design. I'd prefer she thinks of herself as the true grandmother to our baby."

Our baby. It was the first time he'd used those words, and it caused Ruby's heart to fill her throat. He wanted so much to be a father. She could see glimpses of it when he didn't think she was looking. And it was important that he *did* feel that way if he was to play such an important role in her baby's life. Her child deserved a father who would do everything in his power to protect it and love it, not someone who'd walk away from love as he'd done in the past.

"Stella took the news so well," she said, wanting to explore what sort of relationship the two of them might have as mother and daughter-in-law. "I haven't seen her in so long, and I'm sure Mom would've opened up to her about the trouble between us."

He moved the damp cloth to her cheek. "All my mom wants is for people to be happy." He smiled slowly and the expression lit his face. "If she can feed them while achieving that then all the better. Mom's priorities have always been me and Antonia. She'll want to do right by both of us." He drew back and she stirred, missing the low hum of his voice so close to her ear. Missing this caring, protective side of him that made her feel...safe.

"How are you feeling?" he asked.

Sick to her stomach, that's how she was feeling. Sick that they'd lied to Stella, played as if they loved each other when nothing could be further from the truth. But she had to get used to playing that game for people if this was to work. "I'll be fine." She carefully shifted her legs off the couch to the floor. "It's very warm in here."

"You must take better care of yourself, Ruby." He stood and strode toward the sliding doors leading to a balcony and pushed them open. "You hardly touched breakfast this morning, and swimming can't be good when you're feeling faint." Of course that was why he was so concerned about her health—he wanted her to keep the baby safe.

She placed her palm around the curve that was becoming more pronounced in her belly. "Nothing is more important to me than taking care of my baby, Christo, and your insinuation that I'd be careless is offensive. I swam those lengths this morning to keep myself healthy during the pregnancy. I'll continue to do that, and more, to keep healthy for my child."

"Soup, soup!" Stella called as she came in from the kitchen carrying a tray. Christo immediately crossed the floor and took it from his mother.

"You have so much sorrow in your face, Ruby-*mou*," the older woman said as she fussed with a white napkin. "And it is understandable when you have lost your mother and your baby's father. But it is not good for the baby to have you so sad. I want you to think that the baby's father and Antonia are right here with us always. Looking down upon you and knowing that your life will be wonderful with my son."

Ruby nodded as a memory of sitting in the kitchen at home as a ten year-old reeled through her mind. She must've been sick because she could remember the smell of mentholated rub on her chest and the warm, sweet and sour taste of egg lemon soup on her tongue. Things had been so uncomplicated back then. So honest and simple, unlike the tangled web she'd woven for herself now.

She smiled as she looked into the caring face of her mother-in-law to be and gratefully took a bowl of steaming soup.

~

The next evening Ruby drew a deep breath and took one more step forward so she was in Christo's line of vision.

"Ruby." Christo paused for a moment. "You're stunning."

When he'd suggested she accompany him to the ball, she'd worried about what to wear. Now, standing at the top of the stairs as his voice rose to meet her, the butterflies in her stomach threatened to take unanimous flight and send her skyward. Never before had a word stopped her in her tracks like this one. Never before had she wished as strongly that she could hear it all over again.

Clasping the polished banister with a clammy hand, she placed her stilettoed foot on the first stair.

Each step would bring her closer to seeing Christo ready and waiting for her in a tuxedo.

As the stair took her weight, the same squeaky floorboard she'd noticed when she'd first arrived back seemed to underline the stillness in the air and pull tighter at her connection to this house, to the commitment she was making to stay here.

She left her gaze nonchalantly drifting just above his head so she could make it down without tripping. "Thank you." She kept her voice light and breezy, hoping to keep the tremor hidden. "I didn't bring anything formal with me, so I went into Mom's closet. She had some beautiful dresses. This was less fitted than the rest." She faltered and gripped the rail tighter. "I suppose I should go through her things and sort them out." Her throat caught for a second at the memory of her mother, the many times she'd watch her sitting in front of a mirror, gorgeous in an evening dress as she applied her make-up.

She let her fingers graze across the honey-colored silk trailing her thigh, and was instantly calmer. Now that she'd agreed to marry Christo in order to stay in the house, she could take her time in saying goodbye to her mom.

Halfway down, Christo hadn't said anything more, so she filled the empty space, nerves dancing in her chest. "You said we'd only need to make a short appearance tonight, but this is the sort of dress I'd want to stay in all evening long." Still he said nothing, just stood erect, fingers adjusting the cuffs of his jacket, chin tipped high.

As she reached for the last step and he held out his hand, she ordered her heart to resume its beat as his knowing gaze pierced her cool façade.

"It suits you beautifully." His voice was low, his eyes intense and delicious, and Ruby drank in his compliment as a ribbon of warmth unraveled up her arm.

To avoid his gaze, she let her own drift down to his neck where the deep tan of his skin contrasted with the snow white of his wing collar shirt and expertly knotted bow tie, to his chest where the dinner jacket hugged each inch, to the dinner pants that skimmed his thighs.

She swallowed hard and forced her hand to relax in his as she took the last step, and he towered above her.

"The earrings. Are they your mother's, too?"

Ruby absently stroked an ear lobe and watched as Christo followed the movement.

"Yes. I made them for her. They're rose quartz."

Christo nodded and a faint smile lifted his lips. "I remember you making jewelry."

"I hadn't made anything for years, but recently I've begun experimenting again," she said. "I don't ever remember Mom wearing these. I'd forgotten about them." Her heart squeezed. "Dad always wanted to see her in expensive things. There are a few pieces like that in her jewelry box. I guess they should be somewhere safer."

"With you, the baby, and my mother here, security will never be an issue."

A tingle of warmth zipped through her. He was so sure that marrying her was the right decision, so confident that having the four of them living in the house together would be perfect. She'd been thinking about his comment yesterday about his father, and how his mother had done everything she could to keep her own baby safe. *That* was all Ruby needed to focus on now. Her baby.

He turned and led her out the door to the waiting limousine as she regained the breath that had left her. "So, where are we going?" The kiss of early evening air warmed her bare shoulders. Dipping his chin to her, a waiting chauffeur opened the door of the shiny car.

Before she could step forward, Christo guided her expertly inside and ducked his head in to speak. "A charity ball. It's a new education program to get books into the homes of underprivileged children. As I said yesterday, we only need to make an appearance. An hour at most. But you might enjoy re-establishing some publishing connections." His eyes slid across her, and she warmed under his gaze.

She scooted across the plush leather seat, but her passage was interrupted by an ice bucket, the neck of a deep green bottle poking out at a jaunty angle. Tucking her legs in, she smoothed her dress and reached for a lock of hair that had escaped from her chignon.

Christo folded himself into the seat beside her and handed her a seatbelt as the chauffeur shut the door. She looked down, busying herself with the clasp. "I guess it's shrewd of them to invite an entrepreneur. Or is it your famous boy-about-town reputation that gets you invited to A-list parties?"

He let out a throaty chuckle. "Neither of those, this

time." He released a button on his tuxedo jacket and flicked a cuff before turning toward her. "I hope you're better after yesterday?"

Doctor Harlan had agreed that it was probably nothing more than heat and excitement, and she was feeling much better. "Everything's good, thanks."

"Excuse me."

He leaned slightly across her to lift the bottle from the bucket. Suddenly drenched in the cool sea-breeze scent of him, she took a longer breath and pushed her back into the soft leather of the seat. She fixated on the back of his neck as he leaned down. The polished skin there seemed to call to the tips of her fingers to reach out and touch, to stroke.

She tucked her hands firmly under her thighs as the car purred to life. "I've felt fine today," she said. "I spent the afternoon making some calls to old friends in the California publishing industry—one to the publisher of *CeeCee* magazine." She took a solidifying breath. "They want to have a Zoom interview tomorrow."

She watched his face for a reaction as he leaned back, ripped the foil casing off the top of the bottle, and wrestled with the cork. The corner of his mouth quirked. "Ah, *CeeCee* magazine. You'd have spoken to—"

"Don't tell me. You own the magazine?"

He laughed as the cork came out with an echoing pop, his smile flashing in the close confinement of the limousine. "No, not at all. I've worked with Julia Deans a number of times, and she's very good at what she does. *CeeCee* would be a good choice if you wanted to keep on working. But you know it won't be necessary when I'm supporting you and the baby." He poured the fizzing liquid into one of the glasses and waited for her to hold out the other.

"I'm not drinking alcohol, Christo." She held her palm over the rim of the glass.

"This has no alcohol but still has the features of finest champagne. It's one of the new developments from our sparkling wine facility. Perfect for times like these."

He'd organized this especially for her? A smile touched her lips. "Thank you."

She clasped the cool glass a little tighter and set her gaze on his face. "I'd like to keep some independence and not rely on you for everything. My career has been an important part of my life in the last decade, and I'd like to keep some options open." She eyed the glass in her hand. "Wait a minute..." He slowly looked up at her from beneath ebony lashes. "Why exactly are we drinking pretend champagne? Wasn't tonight about me returning a favor?"

He finished pouring, then placed the bottle in the bucket before turning back to her, his voice smooth and playful. "We're celebrating."

"Celebrating?"

His mouth lifted in a candid grin. "Your acceptance of my proposal." He clinked his glass against hers, but she couldn't look at him, couldn't help the feeling of unease that washed through her.

Was this relaxed, affable man the same person who'd stood so confident and resolute beside the pool three days ago? The man who'd said he'd stop at nothing to get her house? Warning bells sounded in Ruby's ears, and she took a sip to steady herself and wash them away. What he'd said to her in the bar about their marriage being consummated flitted through her mind. When he'd first proposed marriage she'd been dumbfounded, outraged. But look at her now. Would it be just as easy to find herself in his arms?

As the fizzing liquid popped and tingled across her

tongue, she let her gaze drift to the beautiful vista beyond the car: Brentwood Bay at dusk, still bright with the heat of the day, always warmed her heart. Staying on guard with Christo Mantazis was a priority. She would not let herself succumb to the charm she knew ran thick in his veins. Everything was moving so smoothly now, and it was precisely at a time like this that she must remember to remain focused. Losing herself to Christo's charms meant she would lose control of what this relationship was. And this time she had more than just herself to protect from the devastating effect of falling under Christo's spell.

7

Although he wouldn't make an announcement tonight—he liked his private life private and would keep their engagement quiet for as long as he could—there was something supremely satisfying about attending this function with the woman who'd soon be his wife. He took the steps two at a time until he was beside her and placed his hand on her waist to guide her through the revolving doors. The instant his skin made contact with the fabric slipping over her middle, he couldn't help but visualize the curve of her body beneath, how smooth and soft that hidden skin must be.

"We'll mix and mingle tonight. A quick appearance." He murmured at her ear as her scent, fresh as honeysuckle, enveloped him.

"You said it was for a reading charity?" A smile touched her glossy mouth. "What a lovely cause. We'd talked about a reading program at the magazine, but it's still in development."

They walked into the huge foyer as the last of a line of people entered the main doors, and Ruby's long legs, even in killer heels, easily kept up with his stride. Moving his hand from her waist to her elbow, he tried to steer her toward a side door. No need to make a dramatic entrance—the tabloids would be sniffing out their arrangement soon enough, and he needed to ensure Ruby wasn't caught up in anything public until the ink was dry on the license. He could still sense some hesitation in her and intended to eradicate that as soon as possible.

"We'll take this side entrance so we're not held up." He was trying to usher her sideways, but she wasn't moving.

Her voice was a breathy laugh, her eyes wide and sparkling—deep-sea blue and gold—and his heart swelled at the vision. "Look at the fabulous entranceway!" He followed her gaze to a line of book character cut outs. "They're huge! There's Tigger, and Harry Potter, and is that Nanny Piggins?"

They were only feet away from the looming door, and he maneuvered himself in front of her. If they went through those doors all hell would break loose. Usually at these things the press was allowed in for the first few minutes only. If they could avoid the inevitable frenzy a public entrance would make, he'd be happier.

"We'll take the side entrance to avoid the crush." He glanced around. Just the two of them left. He pointed to the other door in the distance. "This way, where it's not so crowded."

Silk *shushed* against her limbs as she moved toward him, her face glowing. "I want to see which other characters there are. Oh, look, there's Amber Brown! I'd completely forgotten about those books. I used to read about her until the pages nearly fell out. And Geronimo Stilton. And they've all got little quotes written above. Let's read them."

She drew closer to one of the characters and began

following the trail into the main hall. Chandeliers overhead threw sparkles onto the ground and highlights into her hair. Her face glowed, and Christo groaned under his breath. There was no stopping Ruby Fleming when she had an idea in her head. Her curiosity, her enthusiasm, and her bald stubbornness—they were equally attractive. Always had been.

"Be prepared for some interest from the press as we walk in," he said.

"The press?" She was reading the speech bubble coming from a giant hedgehog and hardly seemed to hear him.

Straightening his lapels, he drew alongside her, his earlier resolve to avoid a flashy entrance evaporated. He was being overly cautious. What did it matter if they came through the main entrance? As soon as he was spotted, there would be some sort of announcement, and then they'd have to pose for photo opportunities. If she was so determined to do things her way, then she'd need to deal with the consequences. And his protection. As his wife, she'd be thrust into the midst of publicity hounds constantly.

Nearing the ballroom doors, a tide of chatter and flirty swing music rushed toward them. Christo leaned in closer and touched her elbow. The sweet scent of lavender shampoo and Ruby got caught with his words, and he stayed where he was and pulled in another breath. "There might be some excitement when we come in. Just smile for the photographers."

She turned her face to him, eyes growing wider as they stepped into the ballroom, and the glittering crowd before them parted. The band stilled, and for an instant there was silence. Suddenly, like cannon-fire, applause broke out, thundering around them and rising louder as it went on.

Flash after flash went off, but Christo couldn't turn from the paleness of Ruby's face, the way her mouth dropped open as she turned to him, desperate for understanding.

"Christo?"

He swore under his breath. He'd avoided telling her this event carried his name. It seemed to offer another complication among their negotiations. But seeing her now, like a rabbit caught in headlights, he questioned his judgment in not telling her exactly what to expect.

"Ruby—" Primal instincts of protection roared through his body and clashed with the small sense of satisfaction that right now she was seeing the *real* Christo Mantazis—the man she'd written off all those years ago. The man who'd pushed himself to number one through strength and self-belief. He tightened his jaw. It was Ruby's lack of belief in him, her refusal to fight for him all those years ago, that had seared the scar that still sat raw on his heart. So why did every part of him want to protect her now?

"The Mantazis Foundation?" she breathed. She stared at words in flourishing script on an enormous banner above their heads. "This is *your* charity? Why didn't you tell me?"

Like leaves in the wind, people came at them from left and right, and before he could answer they were pulled along in a flurry of conversation. He managed to lift a glass of juice from a passing waiter and place it carefully in Ruby's shaking hand. She downed half the liquid in one swallow. When the moment presented itself, he turned his back on the guests milling around them and guided her into a corner.

"Why the secret?" she whispered, her gaze sweeping around them before moving back to his face.

He nodded to the mayor, who lifted an eyebrow and

turned away. He kept his voice low so only she could hear him. "It wasn't a secret. I told you I had a function to attend and that you'd need to accompany me. With the negotiations over the last day, we haven't had a chance to discuss the finer details." He looked over her head. People were hanging back, shooting him questioning looks, but he didn't care. Ruby's attention was fully focused on him, and he wanted it to stay that way. "There will be many functions such as these that you'll be expected to attend as my wife."

She bowed her head, then lifted her lashes. Gone was the dark shock he'd seen earlier; now it was replaced by a look he couldn't name—perhaps approval for what he'd just told her. The expression moved from her face to his body in warming waves. "I'm surprised." Her mouth opened a fraction, and he couldn't pull his gaze from the inviting gloss of her lips.

He let his hand remain a second longer on her arm before he stepped back. She was impressed by what she saw? It shouldn't matter, but the fact he could surprise her, set that spark off in her eyes from something he was so proud of, made him want to do it again. "Surprised that someone as heartless and self-serving as me would run a charity for underprivileged children?"

"No." Her forehead pleated as she tapped her glass on the soft skin of her cheek. "It's...well. Yes, I suppose I am surprised. You said you were an entrepreneur. I didn't imagine you'd have this as part of your life. Did you choose this charity because you'd be helping children?"

He tilted his head to relieve the constriction of his tie. "It's one of my many charities." Again he experienced the sense of satisfaction that she didn't know him at all, but it was joined by the anticipation of showing her even more about himself. "Will you be comfortable, accompanying me to these sorts of events? People will know you're my wife soon enough, and then invitations will include you."

A flush of color crossed her face. "I don't know. It's not something I factored in. Everything's happened so quickly that I haven't had a chance to think about our day-to-day life. Tell me more about the charity."

The set of each muscle in her face relaxed and he reclaimed the step he'd yielded, breathing in her sweet scent, his palm pulsing with the memory of where he'd touched her earlier. "Even though I was the child of an immigrant, I never felt underprivileged. I had my uncle's family, and my cousins, and your family gave my mother a home, a livelihood. But I was always aware that there were other children like me who weren't so lucky. Now that I have the means, I like to do what I can for others. This was the first charity I established."

"It's very admirable," she said, and then her eyes sparked again. "It's something I'd love to be involved in. If that was appropriate. More than just as your wife. Perhaps in a hands-on role."

He dropped his voice further and laid his fingers on the soft skin of her arm. This was all panning out beautifully. "With your publishing background and your father's contacts you'd be an asset to the foundation. I'll put some structures in place for you." Pain flitted across her face at the mention of her father. She was starting to believe the truth he'd told her in the last few days—about her father's deception to both her and her mother.

With one thumb, he stroked her delicate wrist and the blush on her cheeks vanished. For an exquisite moment she held his gaze, her ocean-blue irises shimmering before she lifted the glass to her lips again. "I don't want you overtired."

He touched her arm once more. "We'll stay an hour or two and then I'll take you home."

Three town councilors joined them and he was forced to step away from her, but all the while he watched her movements as she mingled with the crowd. Only when he saw her engaged in conversation with a group of businesswomen did he relax and work through the motions of meeting and greeting on his own.

Half an hour later he stood at the podium, and silence descended. A rainbow of black and white suits and sparkling gowns colored the room before him as he began his customary speech of welcome and thanks, but tonight he kept being drawn back to one woman.

The glint of the crystals in her ears and the way she stroked her throat, head on one side as if she was really listening to him, made Ruby stand out like the morning star. From the way his body tightened, he might've been standing inches from her rather than having yards of distance that caused his speech to quicken, his list of thank-yous to shorten. The need to be back within touching distance was a powerful force that tonight he didn't intend to resist. For the briefest second he considered announcing their engagement—it would be preferable to have the jump on the tabloids—but he wouldn't risk Ruby backing out now in fright. He needed to show her how good life could be with him.

The Master of Ceremonies took over, and Christo automatically sought Ruby again to see if she was clapping as loudly as everyone else. She wasn't. She was deep in conversation, and a twinge of disappointment settled in his chest. When the applause stopped and she still didn't look up, he shook the feeling away and focused on the crowd.

While the MC explained that dinner would soon be

served, Christo strode from the stage and found Ruby. As people moved to the ballroom, he extracted her from her little group.

"It's time to go."

She remained a step away from him, so he closed the gap and took her arm as she whispered, "I've been talking to Tracey, one of your directors, and asking her how I can help out."

He was glad for her interest, yet an overwhelming urge to get away from here, to be alone with her again, took over. "The auction's about to start and I want to put in a silent bid or two. The organizers only expected me to stay a short time. They need to get on with the serious business of raising money."

Lowering her voice, she spoke while her gaze fixed on his. "Do we need to leave now? I'm enjoying myself."

"I can't stay here, Ruby. The focus needs to be on raising money now, not my presence."

She turned to the women on her left and said good-bye.

"Did you learn a lot about the charity?" He took her hand and moved through the crowd.

Cheeks smudged pink, she spoke in a guarded whisper. "A little. The women I spoke to mostly wanted to talk about you. They were intrigued that we'd arrived together."

"Were they now?" He held her closer and allowed the length of his body to soak in her warmth. "Did you tell them you were about to become my wife?"

She smiled. "No, they were very discreet, but I could tell they wanted to ask more about where I fit in."

"They'll know soon enough."

She stopped walking and turned to him, a chandelier overhead throwing sparkles across her shoulders. "Not before I've had a chance to tell my family. We've told your mother, but I'll talk to my uncles before anyone else tells them."

He nodded. "Of course, but as we've done with my mother, you'll need to have them understand that the marriage is legitimate."

She brushed her fingers across her lips and frowned. "I won't lie to my family, Christo. There's been enough deceit in the Fleming family."

"They'll all benefit from having you and the baby in Brentwood Bay." Slinging a hand into his pocket, he continued. "So everyone's a winner."

Ruby watched Christo's easy stance and thought about what the other women had said about him. They'd seemed in awe, as though he were some supernatural being. She'd heard a group behind her speaking in whispered tones about how gorgeous he was, but how aloof and—one of them had said—unchartered. She wondered how many of them would do as she'd done yesterday and agree to become his wife.

A rope of partygoers trailed down the stairs in front of them, and Christo took her arm again. She relaxed into his touch, which had become surprisingly familiar in the last few hours. "This'll take forever," he said. "There's an elevator over this way we can use."

While they walked, she remembered what he'd said about everyone being winners when they were married. He obviously saw himself as one. He'd have the house he wanted for his mother, a baby he would raise as his own, and even a useful wife for his children's charity. She'd also have much to gain in this marriage, but after everything she'd agreed to, how much did he trust her now? And how far would he go in keeping his promise to support her?

As they rounded a corner and left the noise of the ballroom behind, she stopped and turned to him, her hand still on his arm. "I'd like us to be married as soon as possible. In three days if it can be arranged."

Looking around to see if anyone was listening, he backed her into an alcove. "Three days? We can't arrange an appropriate wedding in three days."

She let her palms rest on the sensual silk of her dress and looked him in the eye. "You said yourself that it's the minimum time it takes to get a license. I've decided to return to New York by the end of the week. I need to be sure the house will still be available to me and my baby when I get back. Are you prepared to support me?"

His jaw stiffened. "We can't arrange a proper wedding so quickly. It'll look insincere, rushed. You haven't even told your family yet." His face darkened. "We had this conversation yesterday, Ruby. You can't leave until the contract is secured. Until we're married."

She nodded as her heart rate increased. "We did have the conversation yesterday, but I didn't agree to stay until the wedding. I need to go back now, so I'm offering you an option. Either we get married in three days and then I go, or you agree that while I'm away you won't declare that I've abandoned the house, and we get married when I come back. It's a simple choice."

He fixed her with an impenetrable stare, and she wondered how many others he'd evaluated like this, and how many had succumbed to his will? Stood up to him and won?

She'd been surprised when he'd mentioned a big

wedding yesterday, but now it made sense. He wanted this to look real to everyone.

"I'll come with you," he said. "My PA can organize the wedding and we'll do it when we return."

"No, this is something I need to do on my own. A last good-bye to my old life."

"Planning an escape route in case you change your mind?"

"Christo, if we're to share a house together, a child together, experience good times and bad together, sickness and prosperity, at some point you'll need to trust me. It may as well start now."

He took a step closer, his Adam's apple moving as he swallowed. "That's a lot to ask, Ruby. You used me for effect ten years ago."

She held his stare. He'd really believed her when she'd said she'd only used him to shock her father? They'd been the words of a heartbroken young woman, but they'd obviously found their mark. She fought to contain her surprise at the tension in his voice. "You'd disrespected me and I wanted to hurt you. You can show me some respect by trusting me now."

His eyes scanned hers, and something moved in their depths. He took her hand. "I'll think about it."

As they walked, her heart pounded with what had shifted between them. "I'll be waiting," she said.

They came to a wooden door set into a wall and he punched in a code. "This was one of the first inner city buildings I bought and I retained some of the old features. The council would only let me keep this old elevator if it wasn't left open to the public." Pulling back the door he revealed a highly polished black cage elevator.

She took a step back and let her hand drop. "Are you sure this is safe?"

"Perfectly. I had a whole new mechanism built for it in London. You don't find these much anymore. I remember riding in them when we first came to America. They operate on a simple mechanism, but they're very reliable." He dropped his voice as he stepped closer. "I wouldn't endanger you or the baby, Ruby. Trust goes both ways."

She took the hand he offered and when they were inside he pulled the steel door closed behind them.

When he turned, she became aware of how very small the space was and how much of it his body took up. Her blood began to heat. Could she trust that he wouldn't take a step closer? Wouldn't trap her against the elevator wall so she'd give in to his touch? He watched her as he punched the button for the ground floor and the lift whirred to life.

"It's beautiful," she whispered as she craned her neck to the ornate plasterwork in the ceiling. She wanted to look anywhere but at him to avoid thinking about the two of them in this tiny space. A pulse quickened in her chest and she laid an open palm across her belly.

"Oh," she said, as her mouth dried. She pressed against the far wall, but the ground seemed to suddenly drop away, and her heart was in her throat.

Christo took a step closer. "Are you okay?"

She pulled her tongue across her lips as the dropping sensation intensified.

When he next spoke his voice was closer, a whisper against her cheek, and as she lifted her lashes, he was inches away. "It's the nature of the mechanism," he murmured. "It makes everything swifter, less steady."

The second she shut her eyes, the dropping sensation stopped. When she blinked open, Christo had his hand pressed against the stop button. "We're between floors now. Not much longer. Are you okay?" Concern gathered at the corner of his eyes. "Maybe you're more sensitive to motion now that you're pregnant."

She pulled in a calming breath and smoothed damp palms down her dress. "Thank you." She managed a dry whisper. "I'll be okay in a minute."

"It's a strange feeling. Like being out of control." His voice was a low, comforting rumble. "That's something you and I always had in common, neither wanting to feel out of control."

The skin across her chest heated and she could feel it crawl up her neck. "True." She'd been in this situation before with Christo, when the pull of him had caused her to lose focus, forget what was important.

He shifted his weight so he was a fraction closer, and all air seemed to siphon from the cell-like space. "Do you feel out of control now, Ruby?"

Her cheeks heated and she lifted her chin. He could've been speaking about her reaction to this lift or her reaction to him. Every part of her hungered for him to move closer.

"Say the word and I'll start the elevator again."

In the smallest of movements she shook her head and, as she did, he brushed his knuckles down her cheek. When she reached up to place her hand on his, he dipped his face and claimed her lips.

His warm, solid mouth met hers and Ruby couldn't help herself. Obeying only her body, she pulled him closer, reveling in the strength and surety of him inside the tiny space. As he opened his mouth and his tongue slipped between her lips, she dug her hands into his hair.

His fresh, ocean scent flamed her need for his touch, and

when he walked her back to the solidity of the lift wall it was as if nothing could ever frighten her again.

Every sound around them—her breath in short, sharp bursts, the slide of her dress silk against his fine suit—echoed around and around.

"Christo." She tried to catch her breath as his fingers found the shoestring straps at her shoulders and slipped beneath. "Who are you?" The steely man at the pool when she'd first arrived, the protective son, the charity founder—they all seemed so different, but were all wrapped in the skin that lay so close to her now.

For a moment he said nothing, just drifted his fingers across her arms inch by inch as his gaze bored into hers. "I'm who I've always been."

Her mind swirling in confusion, Ruby dragged his face back to hers and kissed him, long and deep again. Searching the warm cave of his mouth with her tongue, every part of her body cried out to be closer. His kiss, the intensity of him, took her breath away.

Looking up, she was startled by the image in the mirrored wall opposite. She had a view of his jacketed back, her fingers buried in his hair, his hands traveling down her body, and a delicious shiver ran across her skin.

As his fingers curled into the fabric of her dress, she arched her neck, inviting the ribbon of kisses he trailed there. Burrowing her hands under his suit jacket, she slid them across crisp cotton, searching across the rigid stomach muscles—an instrument she could play.

And then, despite her racing heart, her fingers froze.

Everything—the marriage going ahead, securing the house for her child, being unaffected by Christo's presence in her life—depended on her not taking this further. She'd surrendered her heart to him once before. It wouldn't happen again. If she lost perspective and everything came crashing down, they'd all suffer.

She stiffened and he pulled away.

Reaching for the straps that had slipped from her shoulders, she righted herself then brushed away hair that had fallen across her face. "Christo..." She caught her breath. "Could you start the lift again, please?"

"You don't feel out of control anymore?" His breath was warm against her hair.

Her answer scraped the back of her throat. "I think we should go."

He stepped away, and his warming shroud was replaced by cool distance. She busied herself with smoothing her dress and tucking loose strands of hair behind her ears.

"I'm sorry," she said. He stood facing her, back to the doors. "I don't know what came over me."

"Motion sickness?" His lips turned up in a perfect crescent.

"Maybe..."

As she spoke, his head moved in acknowledgement, but the understanding in his face spoke to her. This was about him convincing her that she should give her whole heart to him.

It wouldn't happen. She'd lost all judgment when it came to Christo Mantazis's manipulation once. For her own sake, and for that of her baby, she needed to keep that part of herself out of his reach.

"Thank you for coming tonight," he said. "I think it was a successful evening all around."

With a sudden jolt, the elevator came to a halt. Ruby tugged in a breath as Christo pulled back the door of the shiny black cage, stood aside, and let her walk out first. Of course it was successful. He knew exactly where her weak spot for him was, and she needed to keep it guarded. To keep her baby's family stable, she had to never let him see that vulnerable part of her again.

What she did need to do was negotiate the limousine ride home, endless nights with Christo under the same roof, and the burning understanding that she still wanted him—only much, much more than before.

And now he knew it, too.

8

"What's this?" Ruby asked from the breakfast table the next morning. She put down the china teacup she'd been holding and passed him her phone, her soft expression puzzled.

He read the message that he'd had his PA send her. "Tickets to New York." He passed her back the phone then took a seat. "I thought if you left tomorrow, then you could come back next Thursday. That should be enough time for you to wrap things up. I've instructed my PA to have everything ready for the wedding on Saturday so you'll have enough time to complete the finishing touches. We can't get the Greek Orthodox church at such short notice, so a registry office will have to do."

Ruby gazed down at her phone, then looked up at him. Her features brightened, and he remembered the feel of her body under his touch last night. And it wasn't just her body that had said she wanted him—it burned deep in her eyes as well. She needed to go to New York in the lead up to the wedding or he wouldn't be able to keep from pulling her into his arms at every opportunity.

When they were safely married, when the deal was secure, *then* he would know that this was all possible.

"What made you change your mind about me going?" She picked up the teacup again and searched for its rim with her glossy lips.

"I don't want your attention to be on the opposite coast when my mother's moving in, or when the marriage is underway. Cutting your ties in New York will mean you can give your new life your full attention."

The softness on her features remained, but her tone became more insistent. "And you *trust* that I'll come back as I said I would?"

Unable to look at her soft lips or her easy smile a minute longer, he turned away and busied himself pouring coffee.

Trust. Such a small word caused such a canyon between them. Had she believed him when he'd told her the truth in her uncle's restaurant—that he hadn't been seeing other women ten years ago? His gut clenched. What did it matter? Whether she believed he'd loved only her or not, she still thought he'd been using her to gain status back then.

Not that he'd begun to lose himself in her. Find himself in her.

He gripped the back of a chair. The fact he was using her for his gain now and would continue to do so—for the house, his mother, a son or daughter—would ensure that chasm of distrust stayed rooted between them. "You're the one who needs to be sure about trust, Ruby. Technically you'll have left the house. Since we haven't had time to draw up a memorandum of understanding, you'll be in breach of the terms of the will."

Her cup clinked as she laid it in the saucer. "You wouldn't do that. I know you wouldn't." He turned back, and the furrow on her brow, the quiet confidence in her statement, unsettled him. Had she seen something on his face just now? Vulnerability? Weakness? There was something different about her, as if she'd discovered a crack in his carefully engineered plan, and he didn't like it. Losing his grip on his relationship with Ruby had cost him too much in the past. He wouldn't have her seeing him that vulnerable ever again. "No, I wouldn't have you kicked out. You'll come back as you've said you will, but I don't believe it's from some newfound loyalty to me. You have too much to lose if you don't come back."

"I want this to work, Christo." Her chin was tilted to him, the early morning sun from the French doors behind throwing gold sparks through her hair. This determination in her, the way she could fight for what she wanted, stirred him. "Sharing this house, sharing the upbringing of my child. Trust has to be an important part of that equation."

Trust. No, he'd never trust Ruby Fleming. He'd done that once and she'd come up short. That she'd have stood up for him when her father made his accusations should've been the least he could have expected that defining night. Even if she hadn't felt the depth of connection as he had when they'd said they loved each other, he'd still trusted her as a friend, someone he'd told his deepest secrets to. But she'd been using him for nothing more than shock value and the reality still bit.

Resolution pumped hard through his veins. He would appreciate Ruby as a necessary part of his life, enjoy the sight, the sound, the smell, and the touch of her, but he would *never* trust her. With a woman like Ruby, everything would be fine most of the time, as long as she didn't have another agenda. In those times he could imagine enjoying her company and having a rich life with her.

But if he were to ever *rely* on Ruby, depend that she'd

have his back...that was when the crunch would come. When she'd show her true colors.

He could never afford to forget.

"Anyone home?" As Ruby placed her house keys on the hall stand a week later, she listened for any sound. After the tiring red-eye flight from New York it felt good to be home, lovely to be walking through the front door. Circling her palm against her growing belly, she knew she'd be living here with her baby for a very long time.

It had taken longer than she'd thought to tie everything up in New York and she'd returned a day later than expected. Tomorrow was the wedding, and her head was spinning at everything that needed to be done.

Christo had texted to say he couldn't be at the airport, as this was the day his mother moved back in. He'd wanted the house to be ready for them both. At the sound of movement from the top of the stairs, she looked up and her heart hammered heavy behind her ribs. Christo was coming down from the landing, a white T-shirt stretching across his athlete's chest, faded jeans clinging to his thighs, and weekend-casual hair.

Blood fizzed through her body and she dragged in an extra breath. Memories of the way he'd touched and kissed her just one long week ago soaked through her.

"Welcome home," he said as he took the last stair. "Mom called and said she won't need me for another hour. She's still potting herbs to bring. I could've made it to the airport if I'd known."

Without thinking, Ruby stepped forward, then back. Should she hug him? Kiss him on the cheek? Her stomach swooped. He was about to be her husband, for Pete's sake, and she didn't know how to react to him.

Her uncertainty was squashed as he bent down and picked up her suitcase and carry-on bag before turning to go back up the stairs again. "Good flight?" He spoke over his shoulder, and the lingering scent of soap and Christo invaded her senses.

"Fine, thanks." She took a long, controlled breath, ignoring the unexpected disappointment at his casual response. Roommates. That's what they were. Acquaintances who shared the same living environment. They *would* make this work, because it was the best thing for her baby.

"Is there someone here?" She moved to the stairs. "The Range Rover out front?"

"I bought that for you," he said casually. "You can't live in Brentwood Bay without a car. The keys are in the wooden bowl by the front door."

Her hand flew to her mouth. She began to speak, but he cut her off. "When Mom does arrive, I'd like to give her my full attention."

She blinked in surprise. "Of course. She'll be looking forward to settling back in, I'm sure."

Christo nodded. "I wanted her to move in earlier, but she said she wouldn't be comfortable here without you." He continued up the stairs. "You'll be tired from the flight. Now's a good time to show you our new sleeping arrangements."

Ruby stopped with one foot on the bottom stair, the other still firmly planted on the floor. "Sleeping arrangements?" The shiny banister heated beneath her grip.

Christo kept climbing the stairs without looking back. "What's in this bag?" he asked. "It's making noises."

"Jewelry equipment, crystals, and beads," she said as her

mouth dried. "You've made changes to the bedrooms? Without discussing it with me?" She climbed, one hand pressed to her chest.

"I had one of my builders renovate, but I only changed one bedroom. I'm sure you'll like it. I employed the state's finest young designer, as her taste is similar to yours."

He'd reached the master bedroom, the room she'd stayed in when she first came back, and she caught a breath as he held the door open.

"You've made changes to my mother's room?" Her heart thumped as she stepped inside, and her shoulder bag slid to the floor. It was completely different. Smaller somehow, but far more luxurious. She suppressed a gasp.

"Our room now. The master bedroom." He deposited her suitcase on the king-size bed. "I've moved some of my things into the smaller of the two closets." He stood relaxed, hands low on his hips. "Professional packers have catalogued and stored all your mom's things so you can go through them at your leisure. Her jewelry is in the new safe."

Her hand went to her mouth as she scanned the room. The whole style had changed. What had once been a plain, motherly bedroom was now a place of opulence, with everything made bigger. *Double* everything. Two easy chairs, two desks, two sets of drawers.

In an unguarded moment she imagined this room at night, the twin bedside lamps throwing a sultry light across the huge bed and its luxurious coverlet. Of Christo lying beside her. Then her throat dried. He'd gone back on that part of the deal and expected to sleep with her.

"You can't believe that I'd share a bed with you?" Heat rose quickly from her neck to her face. "We've had this conversation and I explained that's not negotiable. What is it about me that makes you think I'll follow even one of your orders?"

He lifted his chin and gave her an easy smile. "My mom's moving in today. I won't have her seeing us in separate rooms. She'd worry that there were problems between us."

She took a step backward. "We won't share a bed. I won't sleep with you, Christo."

He leaned an elbow on the enormous bureau, and he nodded. "So you've said."

She shook her head. "You agreed, and now you're going back on it. You haven't respected any of my wishes."

"I said this was our bedroom, Ruby. I didn't say anything about sleeping together in it." He walked over to the bathroom door. "I've had this whole wall moved and built another room behind the bathroom. When my mom's retired for the evening, I'll be sleeping there."

While he waited, Ruby crossed the room, her mouth dry. As he held the bathroom door open, she looked into the room beyond. It was furnished in blues and grays. A chair covered in silver fabric sat at a steel desk. This was a man's room. Doors opened to a new balcony.

Part of her breathed easier.

"This is the only access to the smaller room. Mom will never even know it exists."

Sharing a bathroom? An image of Christo, freshly showered, a towel slung low on his hips, caused a shiver to race across her neck, and she swallowed. How could *that* end in anything but trouble? "I trust there's a lock?"

The corner of his mouth hitched. "Bit difficult, considering there's no other entrance to the room. I wouldn't want you to mistakenly lock me in."

Her hands fluttered to her throat. "This"—*is unbearable* —"isn't what I'd imagined. Not what I agreed to."

"What had you imagined? That I'd live out in the servant's quarters as I'd done before? We'll be husband and wife, Ruby. Adults. I'm sure there are many couples the world over who pretend to be sleeping together but who have separate bedrooms."

She crossed her arms under her breasts. "I'll agree to this on one condition."

He said nothing, just held her steady gaze with his.

"We have a separate entranceway built for the new room, and in the meantime I'll take the smaller of the two."

He blinked slowly. "You're worried that I might walk in on you?"

Yes. "I'd be happier in the smaller room."

He sauntered closer, more of his heat soaking through her at every step. He might be saying one thing, but more than instinct said he meant another. For one long moment he looked deep in her eyes, then nodded and left the room.

Man, it was *hot*.

Christo threw off the sheet that had been stuck to his body and swung his legs over the side of the bed. As he scrubbed a hand through his hair, he took a quick look at his phone. 12:30 a.m. One of those Brentwood Bay nights where the darkness beat with heated air. Every breath was a hot, damp effort. Sleep was elusive.

He walked to the double doors leading onto his balcony, threw them open, and took a lung-full of sultry night air. He'd waited a decent length of time before coming to bed so that Ruby would be settled into her new room. The only image he'd had of her since was her lying in her own bed only a few feet from where he stood, little more than a flimsy nightgown separating her from cool sheets.

Throat dry, he padded into his side of the bathroom, and in the blue light thrown from the stained glass window, he found a water glass.

Would there be a nightgown? He turned on the faucet and filled the glass. Or would she have thrown any garment off to lie naked between the linen, her hair a messy halo, a slim hand resting on the curve of her belly? As he pushed the image aside, he turned his face to her door, and his stomach clenched. It was open.

Surely after her defensiveness this afternoon she wouldn't have left it open intentionally. She'd made it clear she wanted to keep her distance.

He should close it. The soles of his feet stuck to the sleek tile floor as he walked across the room and placed a hand on the doorknob.

Was she okay? Maybe the new air-conditioning unit wasn't working. Carefully he pushed the door open and waited while his eyes adjusted to the dim interior. What he saw made his stomach churn. Her bed was empty, sheets flung off, the curtains across her balcony doors open to the night.

Splaying his palm across the wall, he reached with searching fingers until he found the switch and flicked the light on. She wasn't there. In three short strides he'd made it to her balcony to discover Ruby was nowhere to be seen.

She'd definitely been in here when he came to bed. There had been water on the countertop in the bathroom. A drop of sweetly scented moisturizer on a towel. To leave her room completely she must've come back through his room while he was sleeping.

An unbidden image of her watching him sleep coursed through his body. He had to find her.

He threw on a cotton robe and searched the entire house. His mother was fast asleep in her quarters, all the doors were locked, and Ruby's car was in the driveway.

The swimming pool. Of course. His mind swung back to the first day he'd seen her in that white bikini, limbs long and supple. He let himself out the side doors and was soon standing on the pool deck—the slight movement in the water and the damp footprints on the dry wood decking gave her away.

He followed the footprint trail to the summerhouse and opened the door. "Ruby?"

"Christo!"

Standing in a pool of light she was covered in nothing but a white towel, her cheeks pink, mouth open in surprise. Her hair, which had been tied up so often lately, flowed damp and free about her shoulders. A wet bikini lay in a heap on the floor. His pulse spiked.

"What are you doing here?" she asked.

"I couldn't find you." He ordered his vision to move from the curve of her collarbone to the delicate fingers gripping the towel.

With one hand she pulled the towel higher toward her neck. "The heat...I couldn't sleep."

He took a step forward and let the door close behind him. "You're not comfortable in the room?"

"It's fine." The pulse at the base of her throat was rapid. "When I have my own entrance it'll be better."

He stepped closer. "You must've been very quiet when you walked through."

She lowered her lashes. "I didn't want to wake you." Taking up another towel she began drying her hair.

He took a step back toward the door. She was fine. No need to stay. But something kept his feet rooted to the floor as his gaze moved across the room. Somewhere there must be a window open, as he could smell something sweet from the garden beyond.

"I remember this place," he said. It was where she'd made her jewelry. Where her father had found them, in each other's arms entwined. A deep, dark ache arose as that scene came to mind in vivid detail. "Do you remember the last time we were here?"

Ruby stopped, her hair tumbling over one shoulder as she lifted her chin. Silence filled the room, and each one of his nerves pounded with the knowledge of what she'd be thinking about right now.

"I remember the night my father found us, Christo." She looked him directly in the eye, her cheeks flushed. "It was a defining moment in my life."

Something moved across Christo's face as his eyebrow lifted. Surprise? Curiosity? She wasn't sure.

"A defining moment?"

"Of course." Her heart drummed against her breastbone. She twisted the smaller towel into a turban on her head and crossed her arms, suddenly feeling that more than her body was exposed. "That was the day my world changed."

"Because you'd said you loved me, you'd succeeded in shocking your father, and were rid of me in one night?"

She drew her tongue across dry lips. Maybe it was time to get all of this out in the open. They would be married tomorrow, and if they had any chance of making this crazy arrangement work, the future needed to be about looking forward, not avoiding the past that had defined their relationship until now.

"That night," she began, but had to swallow hard to make her voice clear. "That night, Christo, I lost you, and I lost the respect of my father. I was so hurt and angry at you that I wanted you to hurt, too. And it was from those events that I found out the truth about my mother. That night was the catalyst for me to move out of home and to start my career."

He leaned on the doorframe, his gaze dark and intense. "But you said you'd begun a relationship with me to shock your father. Were you lying then or are you lying now? It's one of the two, or maybe both. It's difficult to tell with you."

Despite the cool swim earlier, a new heat rose inside her. A heat that she needed to douse before it overtook all sense and reason. She thought back to her arrival today, to how relaxed and nonchalant Christo had been. Roommates. That's all they'd ever be. "I need to get some sleep," she said. "I'm going back to bed."

He pushed off the frame and, for a moment, the only sound was the chorus of crickets calling from the dark outside. Without Christo moving a muscle, his presence dominated the room, the power of his gaze searching every part of her. If she could leave now they'd be married tomorrow and both have what they wanted. But the pull of him was growing ever stronger.

"It wasn't all bad, was it, Ruby? You and me?" He took a step toward her, his eyes shining in the dim light of the lamp.

She drew in a quick breath to steady the nerves dancing in her stomach. "Some of it was very memorable," she managed.

He was within touching distance, and she couldn't drag

her gaze from the breadth of his chest beneath the cotton robe.

"Was it this that was memorable?" He grazed a finger down her cheek and she swallowed. "Or maybe this." He stepped forward, bent down, and brushed his lips across hers.

Slowly she shook her head, despite her body aching for him to touch her again.

"Perhaps this." He ran his hand down her neck and every thought in Ruby's head scrambled. Why was it that she had to stay out of Christo's arms? What would happen if she succumbed to the seismic pull his body held for hers right now?

Her mind wouldn't provide her with an answer.

"Ruby—" He breathed her name, then pressed his warm lips once more against hers, cupping the base of her neck in his broad palm. Running his tongue along her bottom lip, he pulled her closer, his hand slipping to her shoulders, and her body caught alight.

"Christo." As his mouth moved to graze her throat, her pulse spiked and the promise she'd made earlier demanded to be heard. "We agreed we wouldn't do this."

His mouth formed a smile against her skin. "You said you wouldn't make love when we were married," he murmured, his lips moving to her earlobe. "We're not."

He pulled back for an instant and his eyes, warm and playful, searched hers.

"This doesn't change that," she whispered while one of his fingers trailed down her cheek.

"It doesn't." Did his tone rise or fall? Was it a question or a statement?

When his lips covered hers again she didn't care. When she succumbed to the promise of his kiss, her senses were invaded in one overwhelming minute by the taste, the smell, the feel of his strong, tight body under her searching fingers. She was melting. As her hand slipped under his cotton robe to find the solid wall of his chest, it was as if his essence had been so burned into her all those years ago, and her deepest memory had never forgotten.

But she wanted more of him, the whole of him, his heart, his thoughts, his love. She wanted the overwhelming thrill of being wrapped in Christo's arms. Her mind emptied and the only thing filling her body was the power of him and the burning need to lose herself in him.

The sash windows in the small room were open, curtains puffing in as the hot, moist air rolled in from the night. His breath, soft and warm, made hers hitch. Her mind raced forward to the thought of being under him, part of him.

He took both her hands so they were face to face. Slowly he inched her backward across the floor to the wall, his mouth getting closer to hers with every step as he dipped his face lower. Her feet light on the polished floor, she felt like she was floating and weightless.

Desperate to taste him again, she arched her neck, but he stayed tantalizingly distant, teasing. Each of his fingers laced through one of hers, the edge of his mouth curved down as if his life depended on these next few moments.

With one last step backward, he pressed her into the wall and she waited for his lips to claim her. Mouth heavy with need, she swallowed in anticipation.

But his face stayed inches away, and slowly he lifted both arms above her head and pinned her, palm to palm, only the towel and his robe separating their skin. And then he looked deep in her eyes, and that look, that bone-melting look, sent a whisper directly to her soul. *I want you.*

Christo was strong, confident, and certain of what he wanted, and it caused her limbs to weaken and her lips to open.

"Kiss me," she half-begged. He leaned in and grazed her cheek with his stubble, the pleasure and pain of it shooting beats of desire across her skin. How had she survived so long without him? Without his touch? His warm breath played across her face, and she breathed deeper, wanting every part of him.

With his hands above her head, Christo claimed her mouth, and she searched the depths of his with her tongue. The taste of him was sweet as she played across his lips.

"You're beautiful," he said. Unexpectedly, his fingers stilled. The ring of sincerity in his voice made Ruby's head swim and tears stung the back of her eyes. The pain of wanting him became all encompassing. She bit down on her lip to hold back a cry.

He turned his head and kissed the skin of her décolletage. Above the towel, his lips worked across in fine, feathering movements until, right to her center, she ached for him.

Unable to keep from touching him any longer, Ruby lowered her hands and rested them in his hair. His movements were electrifying as he kissed her back and forth.

She pulled him up and closer until she kissed his perfect mouth. Desperate, she pushed him toward the day bed. The heat from the soles of her feet made her stick to the floor, and her towel lay abandoned.

At the edge of the bed she pushed him backward, further, further, until he was sitting then lying on the soft cotton coverlet. Robe half-open, taut bronzed chest exposed, he looked like a Greek warrior. Her breath shallow, Ruby crawled on top of him, hands supporting her on either side of his face.

Like a triumphant predator, she knelt over him, her heart drumming in her chest, skin slick with desire. Then she stilled. Christo, the man who'd filled her every dream for as long as she could remember, was a touch, a kiss, a heartbeat away, and the beauty of it caused tears to mist her vision as she touched her lips to his.

"Ruby." He whispered her name as he came up for air from their kiss. "I want you more than anything I've ever wanted."

When he pulled her closer, she buried her head in the hollow of his shoulder, heart bursting with impossible emotions. For these quiet, precious moments she wouldn't think about what they were about to do. She'd focus on the feelings flowing through her body and the beautiful man lying here with her.

9

The next morning in the summer house, Ruby stretched a lazy arm above her head, the sun warming the cotton of her pillow, and then sat bolt upright. Her heart hammered against her breastbone. She was getting married today. To Christo. The man she'd sworn she'd keep her heart from. The man who, last night, had made her forget who she was.

Letting out a breath, she sank back against her pillow. How long had she been in the bed on her own? The last thing she remembered was lying in Christo's arms, the scent of gardenias floating in from the midnight garden. The sensation of his strong body wrapped around her branded her memory. The powerful but gentle way he'd made love to her, the unforgettable way he'd held her close... Her chest squeezed tighter, and she could barely breathe.

She'd done what she'd insisted to Christo and to herself that she wouldn't. She'd succumbed to his seductive charm, to his irresistible body, and she'd made love with him the way he'd promised they would. And it had been magical.

Perhaps it had also been a *fait accompli*. Christo had

always known the effect he had on her, and deep down she accepted that this wouldn't be the last time her mind would say no but her body would say yes. Her skin still hummed from where he'd touched her last night. Her lips still tingled from the ecstasy of his kisses.

But what had changed since they'd made love? Today had still dawned bright; the earth hadn't frozen over. On a sigh, she resolved that although she may not be able to protect the will of her body from Christo's power, she could protect her mind—and her heart. Hugging herself tight, she pulled in a breath. *Focus*. That's all she had to do. Focus on her baby's security and happiness, two things she would never trade.

She reached across the bed and pulled a down cushion closer, the curve of Christo's head still imprinted on it. Breathing in the remnants of his male scent, she smiled. There could be many worse things than to share the bed of such a patient and generous lover. As long as she kept that one, beating part of her safe, perhaps—a thrill rushed through her—she could enjoy all of the positives and none of the negatives of being Christo's wife.

Reluctant to leave the serenity of the summer house but knowing she had a hectic day ahead, she formed a makeshift toga from one of the bed's throws and ran the distance back to the house in bare feet. Letting herself in the kitchen side-door, she prayed she wouldn't run into Stella.

"Hello, sleepy-head."

"Hi." Her stomach swooped at the sight of Christo standing at the counter. His hair was damp, he held a coffee cup in each hand, and a broad smile shone on his face. "I've taken my mom a coffee, and I was on my way out to bring you one—and to bring you some clothes." He tracked her shape beneath the thin cotton throw, and her body tingled in reply. He threw her a warm grin. "From the way you were sleeping when I left earlier, no one would guess you were about to be married."

He set the cups down, and in two steps had covered the ground between them and wrapped her in a strong, warm embrace. "If it wasn't for what we had to do today, I'd have stayed longer in that bed with you." He pressed a kiss to her earlobe while his hands caressed her bare shoulders. "But we have a whole lifetime of last nights to look forward to."

For a moment Ruby relaxed into his arms, his breath soft on her neck. Then she lifted her gaze to the carriage clock on the mantelpiece, her mind tripping. "I shouldn't have slept so long," she said. "It's eight. I'm supposed to have hair and make-up done at ten."

"You look perfect the way you are," Christo said, and ran his hand down the flimsy throw. "I'd be happy with just your bed-head and your toga this afternoon." Again he whispered near her ear. "Maybe we ditch the toga."

He smelled of coffee and soap, and she wanted to run her hands along the hard planes of his chest as she'd done last night and sink into the delicious sensations of her body joined with his. Later today she'd see him in a suit at the registry office, declaring that he'd love, honor, and cherish her until death parted them. And it would all be a lie.

"Christo—"

He bent his head and kissed her on the mouth, and she hesitated for an instant before melting into his warm confidence. Her lips tingled with the memory of how and where he'd kissed her in the summerhouse. He drew back and brushed a ribbon of hair off her forehead. "No protests about what we did," he said. "No declarations that it's not what we wanted."

She eased herself back but left her hands resting gently

on his arms. "I wasn't about to," she said, looking up into his face. "Last night was beautiful."

"Then what is it?" He held her closer, and the sure and steady beat of his pulse thrummed under her thumbs.

"I wanted to say that although it was wonderful, I'd like any physical relationship between us to be on my terms." The words came out wooden and distant, and she willed this to be easier than it was.

He grinned and played a slow finger down her cheek. "Your terms? That sounds very clinical. But I like you planning for making love."

She softened her tone. It was so important that she explained her worries, that they keep things clear from this point on. "When we first talked about getting married, you said you couldn't live without sex." She tipped her chin to look directly into his charcoal eyes. "I realize that if we're to maintain a stable home environment for my baby, relationships with people outside the marriage aren't an option."

"Of course," he said swiftly.

She moistened her lips. "Then I want to take a physical relationship between us at my own pace. Figure out what works for me and what doesn't." She paused, tension building in her shoulders. "And for that reason I'd like some rules."

"I like rules." He dipped his chin and laid a kiss on her forehead while his fingers curved around the base of her neck. "Rules can be sexy."

"My bedroom is off limits." She stroked her thumb against the warm skin of his forearm. "I need a place that's private, where I can retreat if things become difficult. It'll take time for both of us to figure out how this relationship will work, and I think some privacy is important."

"No making love in your bed? I can think of all sorts of places I can take you."

As she relaxed, she realized how much Christo's calm and respectful manner meant to her. "And if I decide a physical relationship isn't what I want, you'll respect that, and our arrangement—the way we live day to day—will go unchanged."

Christo nodded and his mouth lifted. "We'll have this written in the contract if it makes you feel more comfortable."

Ruby shook her head. There was something unseemly in that. It was too cold and business-like. They'd moved beyond having every last detail in writing. "As long as we know where the other stands, then I think that's enough. We're adults, we should be able to agree on something like this. It's another point we need to negotiate."

"Negotiating with you could become one of my favorite pastimes," Christo teased as he dragged her close and kissed her.

Ruby pulled her spine straight, smoothed her ivory dress with damp hands, and concentrated on the back wall of the registry office. Chatting quietly behind her were her uncles and their families, Stella and her sister, Christo's uncle Mano and Aunt Mila and some of his cousins, and other people who believed they were about to witness a real marriage between two people who loved each other.

The nerves that had begun when she'd slipped into the dress that Christo had arranged for her were now a full-scale earthquake within her body. No matter how much she wanted to convince herself this was just a contract, the formalization of the agreement she'd made with Christo, it felt like so much more. "It's in all the papers," Patrice, his PA had said. "Brentwood Bay's most eligible bachelor will finally settle down." Her mouth had lifted in a shy smile. "And a few have even suggested Christo's going to be a father."

Ruby had changed the subject then. She wasn't ready to think about what people might say about her baby. Christo had assured her they'd always tell the truth. That anyone who counted would know who the biological father of her baby was. But something gnawed at her. If members of the press were so interested in Christo's private life, how long would it be before one of them discovered that his marriage was nothing more than a convenient arrangement? And how would that affect him and his status as one of California's most successful businessmen? A deep and treasured part of her wanted to protect all three of them and the unconventional family they were about to create.

Christo leaned in, and his cool, ocean-breeze scent caused her pulse to skip. "Have I told you how beautiful you look?" His voice was smooth at her ear, his warm breath causing a trail of sweet prickles down the back of her neck, and it took all her concentration to whisper back as she smiled. "Every few minutes."

She squeezed the bouquet of pink and white roses she held in her lap. These flowers were the only thing she'd had a choice in, but that wasn't the only reason they were so special. They were from the garden that her mother's lover David had tended, and the link between the past and the future was important today.

Patrice had briefed her yesterday about what she'd wear, what flavor the cake would be, and even the words she'd say in the vows Christo had chosen. Then it had all seemed so effortless, so painless—the means to an end that would be the best thing for her baby, and what would let Stella stay in her home. But that was before Christo had taken Ruby in his arms, before she'd opened her body to him once more.

She pulled her shoulders back. Being focused and in control—*that* was the difference between the eighteen-year-old Ruby who'd got things so wrong and this one. Yes, she'd felt all those sensations with Christo before. The way her heart had tripped when she caught him watching her, the taste of his skin as she pressed kisses into his flesh. But then she'd had an unguarded heart and a naïveté that she'd left behind when she'd moved away from here. Now she could let herself feel those things, dream about those things, and know that's all they were—sensations she could acknowledge and accept as part of her new relationship with Christo.

"Maybe the celebrant's been called away?" she whispered. Christo sat beside her, cool and relaxed, his ebony suit molding to his taut frame as they waited.

"This wedding has been organized with military precision," he said with a slow smile. "She'll be here." He dropped his gaze to scan the documents they were about to sign.

As he read the marriage license, Ruby let her gaze drift through a rear window toward the town view beyond, her palm gently covering where her baby lay inside her. It had felt so right, saying goodbye to everything in New York and having all her things shipped here. All she had to do was get through today and then focus on her new life with Christo and her baby.

She pulled her gaze from the window and concentrated on a vase of bright summer flowers on a pedestal. That had been her dream, not her baby's. In marrying Christo she was not only securing her baby's future but also its past. Through what she was about to do now, this little life inside her would be connected to its heritage. It would be safe and secure. Happiness for her baby was her dream now.

Her thoughts were interrupted as the celebrant with a very large pink hat bustled in.

"Good afternoon," she said in a stage-managed tone. "What a glorious day for a wedding!" And then she nodded at them to stand.

Before Ruby could move, Christo reached for her flowers and placed them on the chair beside him, then held out his hand to her. Lifting her gaze to his face, she was sideswiped by the calm confidence in his smile and the warmth in his eyes. For a moment the air seemed to still. Then Christo tucked her hand into his elbow and covered her cool fingers with his. "Don't look so worried," he whispered. "Everything will be fine. I promise. Have I told you how beautiful you look?"

Ruby smiled at him and sent up a silent prayer for what they were about to do.

The ceremony proceeded, fans whirring cool air on them from above, and every time Ruby felt her heart faltering, she reminded herself to focus.

When it was time, she said her vows, gaining strength from the confidence in Christo's replies and in the way he squeezed her hand when she stumbled.

Finally, as they stood facing each other, the celebrant beamed widely and said, "I pronounce you husband and wife. You may kiss the bride." Lightning fast, Christo dragged her to him, and heat flowed across her skin as his lips covered hers, warm, firm, sure. Applause and whoops broke out from behind them while shock, excitement, and unchecked desire rocketed through her. Time stood still.

Unable to prevent herself melting under Christo's touch, she felt her hands twine around his neck, and she pulled him closer, deepening the kiss that should have been all about show and pretense but which felt like a treasure, a gift. The essence of him that she'd had a taste of last night was now filling her senses in every way possible.

10

The following morning, Christo searched the house for Ruby, his stride lengthening with the discovery of each empty room. Since they'd gone their separate ways after breakfast he'd been restless, listening for her movements and wondering where she was. The scent of her from last night still lingered on his skin, but it wasn't enough. He needed her close again.

As he was officially on his honeymoon, it would look odd if he went into the office, and work was the last thing on his mind. The sense of satisfaction he'd imagined when the marriage was completed and the property agreement finalized *was* there, but only in some small part. Odd, considering that for so long he'd wanted to put right what was done to him and his mother here.

The thought of becoming a father was certainly part of the reason that feeling of achievement was lessened. Every time he imagined throwing a ball to his child or helping him or her learn to ride a bike, a sense of completeness overcame him. Whatever the reason for these indefinable feelings, the future for everyone in his newly-formed family was looking bright.

He hadn't counted on one thing, though—the satisfaction in being with Ruby again. Perhaps it was the fact that she appreciated the practicalities of the arrangement as much as he did, or maybe it was the knowledge that they were the perfect physical match.

Overanalyzing anything with Ruby was dangerous. He'd let himself feel too much for her once before—let himself become so distracted by her that he hadn't seen the truth of their relationship. Yesterday she'd said she'd lied about using him, but she'd also said actions were what counted, and her lack of belief in him back then spoke volumes. Keeping things simple, open, and uncomplicated was the key.

He stopped in the housekeeper's stairwell and listened. Ruby was humming softly in one of the tiny sun-filled rooms at the top of the house, and a new urgency to be near her coursed through him. He took the stairs to find her.

"Want company?" he asked at the open door.

Ruby sat in a rocking chair, her head bent over a large tray. She looked up and smiled, the sun throwing a crown of light around her head, and he etched the image in his mind. "Sure," she said. Beside her on a table lay small pliers, some wire, and tiny bottles of brightly colored beads.

"What are you up to?" He stepped into the room and leaned against a large set of antique drawers. The way she sat, bare feet crossed in front of her, flowery dress draped over slim legs, made her look relaxed, content. The thought that she was now his wife sent a shot of pride through him.

"I've been itching to start on a nursery for the baby, but somehow it feels like bad luck." She bent her head once more. "I thought if I put my creative urges into jewelry I might be able to pass the time quicker." She picked up a gun-shaped object and concentrated on a brooch she was holding.

He pulled up a footstool, sat down, then picked up another perfectly round brooch from the table. Delicate pink ribbon spiraled around it, and tiny, lime green beads lay at the center. It reminded him of a bag she'd made when she was younger—a bohemian-looking thing that he'd teased her about though it had suited her perfectly. "I can help," he volunteered as the tip of her tongue poked out from between her lips.

"Sure, if you...owww!" She dropped the gun and sucked at her finger.

He lurched forward. "Are you okay?"

She laughed—a light, tinkling sound—as her eyes sparkled. "Looks like I'm out of practice with a hot glue gun," she said. "Could you please hold this straight?" She held out a piece of turquoise ribbon, the same color as the dress she'd worn the first night he'd seen her again, and he couldn't drag his eyes from her face. The memory of her that night, delicate but defiant, caused blood to pump harder in his veins. How far they'd come since then.

"What is it?" she asked, and he realized he'd been staring at her.

"I was thinking about how surprising you are."

Again she laughed but kept her gaze down as she twisted the ribbon onto another brooch. "What do you mean, surprising?"

He fed the ribbon through his fingers, its slippery softness reminding him of her long hair against his chest when they made love. He shifted on the stool. "At times I think you're nothing like the girl I remember, and then you do things like this—making jewelry again."

She kept focused on the brooch, pulling more of the ribbon toward her. "What makes you think I'm so different from the way I used to be?"

"Because you fought so hard for this house." He watched a blonde ringlet fall across her face.

She stopped for a second as her chest rose and fell, then she tucked the piece of hair behind her ear. "I think I even surprised myself with that. It wasn't until I stood on the front lawn in my bare feet on the afternoon of Mom's funeral that I realized how much I wanted to be back here." She brushed at a damp spot on her cheek, and every cell in his body reared up, ready to comfort her, but she shook her head in the tiniest movement, then picked up the brooch and started work again. "And the more I've thought about bringing my baby up here, the more I'm convinced it's the right thing to do."

"Of course it's right," he said. "This baby will be adored. Treasured. By all three of us."

A soft smile touched Ruby's lips. "I think Mom would be happy to think of us all here together."

"It must be tough being without her, especially at a time like this."

She lifted her gaze to look out the window, and Christo wished she'd turned to him. "Yes," she said quietly. "I find myself wishing that I'd talked to her about things earlier. Made our peace. But I don't want to live with regrets." Ruby placed her hand on the bump at her waistline and finally turned to him. The soft sincerity on her face clutched his chest. "I'm so very glad that she had you and Stella to talk to after everything she went through. And I'm glad we can fulfill her wish for Stella to live here for the rest of her life. I just wish Mom could've met my baby." She stroked her belly. "I have my first appointment with my midwife next week."

"A midwife? Not an obstetrician? I have contacts at the hospital. I'll arrange for a specialist."

She regarded him for a second. "I've chosen a midwife. I've thought about it carefully, and I don't want an obstetrician."

Ruby was keeping her distance when it came to talk of the baby, and it wasn't surprising. It was still early in the pregnancy, and they had enough to do just working out how to live in the same house.

"Let me know the time of the scan." He stroked her small hand with his thumb.

She swallowed slowly, her gaze trained on his face. "You'll be back at work by then. I wouldn't expect you to be there."

"I'll be there."

Her lips lifted in a quivering smile, and when tears began to glitter in her eyes, he squeezed her hand once more.

"It'll be nice to share it. Of course you should be there," she said.

A week later, Ruby pulled into the hospital grounds, parked her car, and stepped out, ready for her first ultrasound.

The rhythm of her life with Christo had fallen into a predictable pattern. He'd gone back to work after a self-imposed honeymoon, and she'd surprised herself by looking forward to him coming home at nights so that they could take a swim together or maybe walk in the garden in the evenings. They'd talked about cribs and strollers, hobbies and sports, and although Ruby had been touched by his level of input and interest, a niggling emptiness had begun to grow inside her, too. This *was* what she'd signed up for when she'd agreed to the marriage, but she hadn't counted on the feelings for Christo that were building below the surface—the way she looked forward to their talks, the way she'd missed being in his arms since their wedding night. Keeping her body from him was supposed to help her have emotional distance. It wasn't working.

On her way to the market, she'd stopped for gas and found a message from the hospital on her phone. They'd rescheduled her ultrasound scan and needed her this afternoon, so she'd hurried straight here, hoping her midwife would be there to meet her.

Christo had been asking all sorts of questions about the scan in the last few days, and he'd be disappointed when he came out of his all-day meeting to find the message that she was on her way. And she was disappointed too.

Taking a path that looked as though it led to the main entrance, she placed a hand above her eyes, and the shape of a man in the distance caught her attention. Drawing closer, her heart thudded. Tall frame, sharp business suit, phone clasped in his hand...

"Christo!" She couldn't hide her joy that he was here. "What happened to your meeting?"

He pulled his signature Ray-Bans from his face and gave her an easy smile. "It's still going. I told them I had a more important place to be."

Ruby focused on the relaxed set of his features, and a sense of warm relief played through her. It would be such a special moment—the first time she saw her baby—and she'd only ever imagined it with her mother beside her, and when that wasn't to be, alone. Having Christo share it with her would make it even more special. Something they could talk about in years to come.

"We'd better go." His palm found the familiar place on her back, and instinctively she relaxed. "We don't want to be late. Are you comfortable enough? I Googled baby scanning and it said you needed to drink a ridiculous amount of water before they could screen you."

"I'm fine." Ruby smiled. "That's only for the optional early scan. What with everything that was going on those first few weeks, I didn't schedule one."

They walked through the automatic doors and headed to the elevator.

As the doors slid open and then closed behind them, Ruby was caught by a potent memory of Christo's lips on her neck, and of her fingers tangled in his hair the night of the ball. An unbidden bolt of desire coursed through her as he leaned against the elevator wall and watched her while the car began to move. His whole body had become so familiar to her since that day, and she was missing it. Missing the exquisite sensations as he caressed her skin, missing the way he moaned her name when she caressed his, missing the powerful and frightening connection when he looked into her eyes as their bodies joined. But they'd become closer in other ways, in the soft security of day-to-day life, in the predictable comfort of a new, uncharted type of relationship. Now it felt dangerous to mix the two.

"I've arranged for us to meet with one of the country's top obstetricians today," he said. "She'll give us all the information we need."

Ruby stood straighter. "I have my midwife, Christo. I'm very happy with her care, and I won't be changing."

He slung a hand in his trouser pocket. "The midwife won't be required anymore. Dr Glazer comes highly recommended and will provide the best care for you and our child. I'm not taking any chances."

A tightness began behind her breastbone, and she had to steady her breathing. She'd seen that ruthless, take-no-prisoners look on his face many times before, but she'd foolishly believed they were working together now—that since the marriage they'd work at respecting each other's needs. Christo obviously didn't see their relationship like that at all.

She clasped her hands together. "So you organized all this today? With total disregard for my wishes? You've made the decision about my medical care *for* me?"

"For you and the baby."

She let out a tight breath. She'd allowed herself to be maneuvered and manipulated by Christo out of necessity these past weeks, but this was going against her express wishes. He still didn't trust her or her judgments. He was removing himself, running away from communication and compromise as he'd done before, and it caused her blood to chill.

She lifted her chin. "If you're concerned, I'd expect you'd at least consult me before making decisions about my welfare."

Christo leaned against the wall of the elevator. "I want to be fully involved in this baby's life, Ruby. And if that means making a call on what's best, then I'll do it. Whenever I need to."

She placed a steadying hand to where a pulse drummed in her throat. "What about *my* choices? When, in any of our *negotiations*, have you considered what *I* want?"

He lifted a strong shoulder. "You won't need to choose. I'll always give you the best."

Her jaw ached with the effort to suppress her anger at his cool dismissal of her. This arrogant sense of entitlement, his idea that he would always do what was right and that she never would, burned inside her. "You honestly think the best thing for our relationship is to make decisions without consulting me?"

"Our relationship? You mean our *arrangement*."

Heat rushed to Ruby's cheeks at his correction.

"Honesty is what will get us through in this arrangement, Ruby, and I'm being honest about what I require. We're a realistic couple, and we'll be a realistic family," he said as the elevator announced they'd arrived at the right floor. "We can be honest."

A realistic family. The words sounded again in her mind, sending a chill down the back of her neck. This was all so practical and convenient for Christo, and for her and her baby. But families were so much more than practical arrangements, convenient connections between people. It was fine that Christo saw the two of them as being a realistic couple, but what about her baby? If he couldn't love *her*, couldn't respect *her* wishes, couldn't *communicate* with her, then how could he ever really love her child? Ruby took a steadying breath as reality, cold as a metal blade, sliced through her.

She blinked and shook herself as they walked toward the reception desk. With the best intentions in the world, she'd committed to a life with Christo and she had to make the best of it. Find a balance between her physical need for him, the undertow of desire for something so much more, and the cold truth that he'd never trust her. She'd stand her ground about her midwife. Not here, not now, but Christo would know there were some things that were *not* negotiable.

Half an hour later, Ruby was lying on her back in a dimly lit room as Christo stood in the shadows. His cell had rung while they were waiting, and the radiography receptionist had looked over her glasses at him with a frown. He'd thrown her his charming smile as he flicked it off, and she'd blushed pink.

"Come closer," the sonographer was saying to him. "You won't have a good view of your son or daughter from there."

He came closer and took a seat by the bed. Ruby watched him fixate on the blank ultrasound screen.

"Is this your first scan, Mrs. Mantazis?"

"Yes." Ruby turned back while the woman switched on a monitor. Her palms dampened as anticipation grew. She couldn't wait to see her baby—the little life she'd fallen so deeply in love with already.

"We'll be measuring different parts of the baby today to determine your due date and to check that all growth is normal." She lifted Ruby's blouse and smeared some clear gel on her belly.

As the sonographer took a seat and picked up her equipment, Ruby stole a look at Christo. He was staring intently at the screen, his hands clasped beside her on the bed.

The woman smiled as she held the instrument above Ruby's belly. "Let's take a look."

The screen in front of him flickered, and Christo shifted his gaze to the wide-eyed look on Ruby's face. Her glossy lips were parted, and her graceful neck twisted to get a better look at the screen beside her. Every day he caught her with a different expression, and, as her body changed with pregnancy, her movements became slower, her smile softer.

There was something else about her that had changed. From the closed and grieving woman he'd seen that first day in the swimming pool to the open and tender one he saw now, something had shifted.

Then he realized what it was. For the very first time since he'd seen her again, it truly hit him—Ruby was going to be a mother. And he was going to witness the beauty of it unfolding. Each day they'd cope with the challenges ahead, learn, and make mistakes together. Knowing how hard she'd fought for this baby already, that she *did* have the capacity to stand up for someone she loved, caused a rock of emotion to block his throat. He swallowed it away. This situation was as it should be, just as they'd agreed. These feelings for Ruby were part of the natural evolution of their arrangement, nothing more.

"Are you comfortable?" he asked as the other woman swiveled to type something into a computer. He shifted a pillow under Ruby's head so she could see the screen better.

She nodded, a slight frown marring the skin of her forehead. "That's fine."

He moved closer. "You don't look fine," he said, touching her arm. "What is it?"

She bit down on her bottom lip and lowered her voice. "I've been so excited about having this scan that I haven't prepared myself for if the news isn't good."

"Of course the news will be good." He took her hand in his. For the first time a seed of worry burrowed into his own mind, but he shook it away. As each day went by, he'd imagined the moment when he'd meet this child for the first time. The day this little boy or girl would call him Daddy. He wouldn't entertain the idea that anything could be wrong.

Ruby's skin was cool, so he placed his other hand on top to generate some warmth. "Dr. Glazer will give us the results as soon as this is over."

She turned luminous eyes to him, and something kicked deep in his chest. "Christo, I need you to listen to me." She took a breath and seemed to search for the right words. He squeezed her hand and leaned closer. Did she have bad news already? His chest hollowed.

If he lost this baby he'd lose Ruby...and he couldn't let that happen again. The thought came from nowhere and struck him hard in the chest.

He breathed deep, focused on the hand beneath his, and pushed the feeling aside. This baby needed him to be strong, not weak as he had been when he'd felt this way about Ruby before.

"What is it? What's wrong?" he said.

A small frown creased her brow. "You have to trust my judgments and respect my wishes. We can't work together for this child if one of us is making all the decisions." She rolled a little closer on the pillow. "Christo, if this is going to work, you need to trust me and the things I want for myself and the baby."

He leaned back in the chair, caught by the challenge in her stare, and swallowed. Suddenly the feelings of a moment ago were brought into sharp focus as what she was asking hit home.

Trusting Ruby meant letting go of the bands he'd so carefully crafted around his heart. The bands that had started to slip in the last few moments. It would mean believing she'd fight for him if he needed her to again. And although he'd witnessed her capacity to fight for someone she truly loved, she'd done nothing to make him believe she would ever do it for him.

He paused a moment and leaned closer, the strength and determination that had rewarded him in life so far coating his words. "I'll give you the best of everything, Ruby.

The best home, the best medical care. I've promised you that. The best. That's all I have."

Suddenly the room was filled with a *woosh-woosh* sound and Ruby's eyes widened. "Is that the heart beat?" she asked, twisting back to the screen.

"Yes, it is," the woman said as she pushed a button, and one part of the screen was magnified. "There's your baby's heart," she added, pointing. "And it's beating beautifully."

Christo swallowed. His attention was glued to that tiny square of information. A heart beat there. The heart of the little boy or little girl who he'd see grow up. This was the heart of the child he would protect as fiercely if it carried the same blood as him. Under his touch was the mother who was nurturing that child. The woman he would share parenthood with. The perfection of the moment caused breath to seize in his chest.

"Does everything look okay?" Ruby asked the sonographer.

"Looking great so far," the woman said as another image illuminated on the screen. "There's a thigh bone. Looks like this will be a tall one by these measurements. Might have your height, Mr. Mantazis."

Ruby's gaze moved to Christo's, and the lines deepening on her forehead showed concern for the woman's question —her natural assumption that he was the biological father. "If it's lucky it'll have its mother's looks," he said, smiling at Ruby.

"Would you like to know whether you're having a boy or a girl?" the sonographer asked them both. "I can tell you if you'd like."

Ruby's sparkling eyes shot to his. "Are you happy to wait for the surprise?"

"Of course." Christo returned her smile. "A few months

ago I wouldn't have believed I'd have to make a decision like that. Waiting a little longer is fine."

As the sonographer continued the scan, answering the questions they asked and reassuring them that everything looked fine, Christo couldn't suppress the tangle of emotion inside him.

Yes, he had a secure future for his mother, a wife to share his bed, and the birth of a baby to look forward to. But now there was something more. A growing realization that Ruby was affecting him, slipping through the cracks in his defenses, and sliding into the secret places of his heart. And when Ruby started to reach his heart, that's when she'd pull everything out from under him.

To protect the things that he'd fought so hard to come by, he needed to stay on guard.

"Goodnight, Stella," Ruby said as her mother-in-law kissed her on both cheeks.

"Sleep well, Ruby-*mou*." The older woman stroked Ruby's face with work-roughened hands. "And goodnight, my little one," she said as she blew a kiss at Ruby's stomach. "You were beautiful on the television today." Ruby smiled at the memory of Stella, transfixed by the video of the scan they'd brought back from the hospital. It felt good to have shared this special time, but uneasiness built inside her.

Christo looked up from his laptop at the kitchen table and smiled at his mother as she walked past. "*Kali nichta*, Mama. Will you be ready to welcome the new household staff when they arrive at nine tomorrow?"

"Tsk, tsk." Christo's mother shook her head. "I told you it

isn't necessary. I have been the housekeeper here for forty years. How you think I will spend my days now?"

"Relaxing, Mom. That's what you should be doing now."

"Hmppff. Teaching them how to do things properly. That's what I'll be doing."

Christo chuckled as his mother bustled from the room. He looked so relaxed in a cotton T-shirt and jeans. Everything about him looked comfortable, from the slightly messy hair to the cover of dark stubble at his chin.

"You look tired," he said to Ruby. He closed his laptop and stood. "I've had some reports done on where's best to make early school enrollments, but I can take you through it tomorrow."

From where she stood in the kitchen Ruby couldn't conceal her shock. "You want to complete an enrollment before the birth? For a place in five years' time?"

He moved to the breakfast bar. "Of course. Waiting lists for the top schools can be decades long."

She swung around to face him. "But we don't even know if it's a girl or a boy yet."

"No matter. St. Bartholomew's is the best boys' school, and St. Augustine's the best girls'. Some well-placed donations now will secure a spot in either."

Ruby switched off the kettle and drew a cup toward her with shaking fingers. "You're doing it again, Christo. Making decisions without me. Not even asking my opinion, just as you didn't ask about my midwife. How can we ever progress to a relationship resembling anything normal if all you do is shut me down?" Every time he did this he was removing himself from her, running away from any chance at a real connection instead of standing with her and communicating. It was what he'd always done, and the frustration of it rolled in her stomach. "I went to a co-ed school," she said. "And you went to a state school. We'll consider those."

"If they're the best options when our child is ready, we can change. And what could be more normal than two parents discussing their child's schooling? I can see you're too tired to discuss this now. Tomorrow will do."

She leaned against the counter, frustration at his dismissal of her again causing the edge of her tone to harden. "You not trying to dictate every little thing without discussion would be more normal. If you tried to show the tiniest amount of trust in my opinions, in my desires." She blew out a breath. "In me."

He was right. She did feel tired, but not the sleepiness she'd experienced in the early part of her pregnancy. This was an all-encompassing tired, a bone-weary fatigue that slowed every thought and left her feeling empty. And it was getting worse day by day. Every hour she spent with Christo in this house, the feeling increased. It was sucking the life from her.

Every time he spoke about their future, every time he touched her, something inside her died. While she had so much to look forward to—the house, her baby, the security Christo offered—a crack had formed in her heart, and it was getting wider by the day.

He moved to where she stood in the kitchen. Did the frown that reached his forehead indicate she'd reached some part of him?

"I do think you want what's best for this child," he said. "How could I not, when you've clearly decided to put him or her first by staying on in this house? But there are certain things I feel strongly about, and education is one of them."

She put down the cup of herbal tea she was drinking. Part of her wanted to leave and go upstairs now, pretend everything was fine. The part that ached for a *real* connection with Christo—attempting to find if any part of him could ever trust *her*—won over.

"It was good having you there today," she said as she looked into his face. "It meant a lot that you wanted to see my baby. But can you imagine what it feels like to have my wishes trampled on, my decisions marginalized? Like I did when you removed my midwife today?" She tilted her chin. "I'll be calling first thing tomorrow to reinstate her."

He paused for a second, ignoring her declaration, and his gaze became more intense. "Now that we're married, I was hoping you'd start to think of it as our baby. We'll share all aspects of parenting. I won't shy away from diaper changing or getting up to help with night feedings. And the specialist was the best option. Surely you can see that?"

Ruby pressed her lips together. She hadn't reached him at all. They might be able to share the parenting of this baby, but they could never be a *real* family. She saw that now. Christo might be able to buy her agreement to share this house, he might even be enthusiastic about raising a child, but if they weren't a *real* family, a really *loving* family, how could they truly share anything? What sort of a lesson would it be for a child to see that its parents didn't truly love each other, couldn't even *trust* each other? She'd been so naïve to think Christo could believe in her. The dread that had been a whisper at her scan today was beginning to grow into a leaden weight within her.

"You're a beautiful mother," he said suddenly, and she looked up into his endless ebony eyes before he took a step closer. "Seeing your face as you watched that ultrasound screen was unforgettable. We're doing fine. You shouldn't worry so much."

She twisted away and busied herself folding a dish

towel. Her body ached for his touch, but this new sense of understanding tore at her will. He placed a hand at her neck and pulled her close. "And I like what pregnancy does to your body." Ruby placed her hand on his arm and looked up into his face, searching for a clue that she was wrong, that he *could* have feelings for her. A sign that he could love her as more than just the woman he'd live with and the mother of his child.

All she found was desire for her body, for the undeniable physical connection they'd always had, and she closed her heart to the warnings whispering in her ears. He dipped his face closer and she found her lips searching for his. This was all he'd ever offered her, all she'd said she wanted, and for now it had to be enough. Closing her eyes, she let her body do what it did when Christo called for it.

When she didn't find the warm comfort of his kiss, she opened her eyes to find his gaze fixed on her face. "I've tried to respect your request that you call the shots on our physical relationship, Ruby, but your signals aren't always clear. Is this what you want tonight? It's completely fine if it's not. No pressure. Ever."

"Yes. In the summer house," she whispered. It was everything she wanted, but not in the house, not where it could mean too much. "Meet me in the summer house."

"No." His hand slid further to her waist, then her hip.

She lifted her lashes, her heart pumping hard. When she made love to him this raging river of doubt would leave her mind, everything would, except the essence of Christo, and she was ready to make it happen again.

"No more secret sex, no more love making in the shadows, Ruby. Tonight I'll make love to you in my bed." And in one swift move, one hand was around her back and one under her knees as he lifted her into his arms. "The benefits of being a retired gym trainer," he whispered in her ear, "means you can whisk a beautiful woman up the stairs at a moment's notice."

Ruby's heart sprinted as he climbed the stairs. "We said no bedrooms, Christo." Panic that this had all suddenly changed raced through her. His bed? All night? That would mean so much more than an hour or two of passion in the summer house or a stolen moment on the couch.

He paused on the stairs and hugged her closer so that his breath warmed her ear when he whispered. "*Your* bedroom. I believe that was the rule." Then he kissed her, long and slow on the mouth, and her whole body melted.

The solid wall of his chest molded her body to his as he continued to climb. Fighting the urge to resist again, she dipped her chin to rest her head on his shoulder, the beat of her heart keeping time with his. When they reached the bedroom door, he kicked it aside with one foot and took her to his bed.

Carefully he lay her on the cover and, ignoring every warning in her ears and every trip of her heart, Ruby's body responded the way it always did. Her head tilted back, ready for the string of kisses he'd place there. Her back arched so she could be closer to every part of him, and her fingers moved across the crisp cotton of his shirt, aching to connect with the skin that hid beneath.

"Look at me, Ruby." His voice was seductive, smooth. When she tilted her face down, he claimed her mouth in a hot and unrelenting kiss. His warm tongue swept across her lips. The movement was so swift it took her breath away, and she reveled in the taste of him. "The summer house is beautiful," he said as he laid a reverent kiss at her throat. "The couch, sexy." He laid another kiss beneath her hair. "But there's so much more room for making love on this bed." He caressed the skin where her shoulder dipped. "And there's something very sexy about making love to my wife in my bedroom." His voice rumbled in her ear as his lips followed the line of her chin. His hand slid down her body. "I want each time we make love to be more memorable than the last."

Ruby bit her lip. Nothing made sense anymore. The feelings that blossomed inside when he touched her like this shouldn't be part of a practical arrangement. They couldn't be healthy in a relationship without love or trust. But she didn't have the will to stop him now.

Christo's face was bright, smile open and broad. No hint in him of the battle raging through her own heart, none of the confusion chilling the warmth his touch had left on her body.

In his face she saw that, for Christo, nothing had changed between them in the last few weeks. Making love to her would be for nothing more than his convenience.

And that's all their marriage would ever be.

A marriage of convenience.

11

In the dim light of the bedroom, it took Ruby a moment to register where she was. Then she remembered. The warm, strong arms holding her close, the fingers splayed across her swelling belly, the soft, sleeping breath at her neck: the essence of Christo burned into her every pore.

She was in Christo's bed, her body spent from making love to him half the night, and her heart now ached from the realization she'd come to. This precious, fragile knowledge had begun as a whisper, a glimmer that grew brighter the more she tried to ignore it. She was sick of pushing it away, squashing it, denying the overwhelming and heartbreaking reality. She was falling in love with Christo.

She focused hard on the wall in front of her, at a spot illuminated by moonlight from the window, as a hot tear trailed unchecked down her cheek.

This was the way it would always be for her. Playing house by day and making powerful, unforgettable love by night with a man who'd keep her at arm's length, who'd never trust her. This man was generous and caring, deeply passionate and driven, but he'd always said he could never have a real relationship with her. Christo would remove himself from her, emotionally and maybe even physically, when the going got tough.

Another tear fell on her lashes as the ache expanded in her chest. Since she'd come back to Brentwood Bay, she'd been so focused on securing one thing—a family home for her baby—that she'd ignored something far more important. Spending her life and sharing her baby with Christo wasn't enough. Not when she felt like this. Now she wanted so much more than what he'd already given her.

She needed him to *love* her, too. A sob began at the back of her throat, and a sharp pain built behind her breastbone as she tried to stem the tide of tears that threatened to spill.

She let her fingers trail down to where Christo's hand lay and gently covered it with her own. It wasn't a house and financial security this baby needed. Not just a father figure to provide it with a well-rounded upbringing. What her baby needed was a family where the father and mother loved each other. *Trusted* each other. A family where her little girl or boy not only believed that it was deeply loved by both parents, but that it was part of a loving family. Gently, so gently, she squeezed Christo's hand, and when she felt his warm, smooth wedding band—the heart breaking symbol of their sham marriage—a part of her heart crumbled.

It didn't matter if she loved Christo. If he didn't love her, then they could never be the family that she wanted. There was absolutely no doubt that Christo would do his best to provide for her child, but he was used to getting what he wanted and having others behave the way he wanted. He'd brought her and her baby into his life for convenience, not for love. In the last two days, she'd seen that he didn't have faith in her ability to make the right decisions. He didn't feel they could discuss what was best for her baby.

But he *could* have a real family, when he met a woman whom he truly loved. A woman he could trust. Her lip trembled at the beautiful image of him as a loving husband. Maybe he'd adopt, or investigate other avenues. If Christo wanted to be a father, he'd find a way. When he fell deeply in love with someone, he'd create the most beautiful family. His generosity, his fierce belief in protecting those he truly loved, convinced her of that.

She lifted her hand and swiped at another tear. Of course she could stay in this house, being cared for, having every material thing she wanted, having a gorgeous man make love to her every night. But it wasn't enough. She wanted to be with someone who loved his family in every way possible.

She needed to be with someone who loved *her*.

Easing herself from Christo's grasp, she heard him sigh as he rolled over. His broad back now faced her, and her heart broke a little bit more. She would always be grateful for what he'd done for her, but for her own sanity and for the long-term emotional security of her child, she needed to leave. And she needed to do it now, before anyone else got hurt.

Cheeks damp, heart leaden, she pulled on a light cotton robe and quietly let herself out the door. With a few phone calls she'd be out of this house for good. She'd be out of Christo Mantazis's life, and on the path to starting her own.

~

"Ruby?"

An hour later Ruby looked up from where she sat,

exhausted, at the kitchen table. Lists of what she needed to do next were fanned in a random pile. And the sight in front of her caused blood to stall in her veins. Christo stood in the doorway, nothing but sky blue boxer shorts and an open cotton robe covering the tanned expanse of his body. His hair was sleep-mussed, and he was rubbing a hand across his stubbled chin.

"Are you feeling all right?" In a second he was at her side, and her senses were filled with the musky scent of warm body and lovemaking. He frowned. "The baby?"

Focusing on the darkened shadow of his chin, she shook her head, struggling to keep her voice steady. "It's fine. Everything's okay with the baby."

He pulled up a chair to sit down, and she wished the night wasn't so hot so that he'd pull the robe across the chest she'd snuggled into only hours before. She squeezed her eyes shut against the image.

"Then why are you up at 2:00 a.m.?"

She pulled in a steadying breath, her heart beating roughly in her throat. "I'm moving out." She opened her eyes and looked into his face. "I'm ending our marriage."

His jaw set firm, and he placed an arm on the table in front of him. "You want a divorce after a month?" His black eyes flashed. "After what you just did to me upstairs?"

The memory of his touch still branded her body; his whispered words of desire still sang in her ears. "Yes." She swallowed hard past the sadness blocking her throat. "We can do it discreetly. Explain to everyone, to Stella, that things didn't work out. It's better that it happens sooner rather than later."

For a moment, the only sound was the ticking of the old carriage clock on the mantelpiece, and then Christo spoke, his voice flat but calm.

"And *how* did things not work out?"

She raised her chin, and his gaze hooked her as an answer died on her lips. A great, gnawing ache deep in her chest threatened to stop any more words passing her lips.

"You have a share of the house as you wanted. Security for your baby as you wanted. I haven't reneged on my side of the deal."

You made incredible love to me, Ruby thought. *Every time more special, more exquisite than the last. And I thought I was strong enough to accept it as another part of our practical arrangement, but I'm not. I need so much more.*

"You haven't reneged on anything, Christo." She spoke on a sigh. "This would be so much easier if you had. You've done exactly as you said you would. But I've realized I want more than you can offer me."

He dragged his chair closer, a look of cast-iron determination shadowing his features. "More than the return of your family home? More than a secure future for your child?" His voice grew tight. "More than all your expenses paid and a generous allowance so you don't have to work? More than a built-in grandmother who'll love your child like one of her own?"

"Yes," she whispered. She held the confusion in his gaze, her heart sprinting as the reality of all she was walking away from was spelled out to her. "I'm sorry, Christo. I know I agreed to those things in the beginning, but I've realized I need more. I want a *real* relationship with a man who loves me. Someone who'll be emotionally present in the good times and the bad. It breaks my heart, but you aren't that person." She placed her hand on her belly. "I need to do this now before someone gets hurt."

He pulled back in his seat as if he was suddenly fully awake. "This makes no sense."

"I'm moving out tomorrow, and I'd appreciate it if you didn't contact me for a while so I can readjust." The chasm in her chest grew wider, and the tears blocking her throat grew hotter. "I'm so very grateful for everything you've done. Truly."

His eyes were fixed firmly on her face, his voice hollow. "Where will you go? Back to New York?"

Her mouth dried, and she rubbed fingers against her pounding temples. "I don't know yet. I'll find somewhere for the two of us."

"Where?" His tone was so gentle it almost unhinged her. She'd expected him to be angry, or at the very least upset. "Can you afford to buy a place of your own?"

"I haven't thought the details through completely." She caught the waver in her voice.

"So that's it?" He leaned back, and a harder tone edged his words—the same tone she'd heard on her first day back here. She shivered. "We come to an agreement and then you suddenly change the rules?" This was more what she'd expected, and somehow it relieved her. It masked the grinding ache in her chest a little.

"I haven't changed the rules, Christo. I'm not the same person I was when I signed that agreement or made those vows. Since I've spent time back in this house—and time with you—I've realized that I need more than you can offer me. More than a life where you make my choices for me." She clasped her hands together on the table, willing her voice to stay steady. "I've already called my lawyer in New York and instructed her to sign my share of the house over to your mother. I'm going to follow through on my mother's wishes as I probably should've done all along." Her voice cracked, and she took a breath. "I hope you'll both be happy here."

"What do I have to do to get you to stay?"

She paused for a moment as her stomach swooped, knowing that when she said this she couldn't take it back. "Say you can offer me the whole package. Everything a husband should offer his wife. Acceptance, trust, forgiveness. *Love.*"

A shadow passed across his face, and a muscle in his jaw pulled tighter. He took a moment before speaking. "The fact that I offered a compromise on the house demonstrates my acceptance of what happened between us before." He scrubbed a hand across his chin. "Forgiveness, too, I guess."

Ruby concentrated on steadying her trembling lips. "You still don't trust me or my decisions. You remove yourself from communication when you should be standing beside me, talking things through with me. And you can't offer me love, can you, Christo?"

He sat still for a moment and then leaned further back in his chair. The pained look on his face could've been enough of an answer, but the silence rammed home harder.

Even though she'd known in her soul he felt that way, she couldn't prevent the arrow to her heart. She couldn't stop the hole that caved inside with the knowledge that he'd never love her, and that she'd never lie in his strong arms again. She couldn't seem to fill her lungs with enough air as reality pounded through her.

She shifted her chair back, desperate to get away from the look of resignation on Christo's face.

He shrugged a strong shoulder. "We share a home, soon we'll share the upbringing of a child, and I know you enjoy sharing my bed. Why do you need more?"

She shook her head and blinked away another tear. "I want so much more for my child than just a beautiful home to grow up in, Christo. I want my baby to never question its part in a loving, committed, *trusting* family. Since I've been back here, I've begun to understand the niggling feelings I had as a child that something was wrong with my family, that something was wrong with *me*. My parents didn't love each other; they didn't trust each other. They both lived a lie to get what they wanted, and I'm not prepared to do that to my child."

He sat in silence, shoulders rounded.

Part of her ached to reach out and touch him, to establish one final moment of togetherness before she left. She laid a hand on his arm, and the bittersweet realization that this could be the last time they touched sent fresh tears to her eyes. "I'll always be grateful for what you've done for me," she said, every word an effort. "And when you do fall in love with someone, I hope with all my heart that you'll have the chance to be the fantastic father that I know you'll be."

When he said nothing more, Ruby turned and walked from the room, finally letting her tears fall.

"Christo, it's all over the papers. We have to do something, or the public support of the charity will be finished. At the very least you'll need to make a statement."

"It's nobody else's goddamn business," Christo ground out. He turned his back on George, his media relations manager, and glared out his office window to the glittering harbor in the distance. He'd spent the last week honoring Ruby's wish that he leave her in peace, and every day this tightness in his chest had increased until it was a permanent, pervading ache.

Where was she? *How* was she? And now that their separation had hit the newspaper headlines, would it be some rabid journalist who'd know the answers to those questions better than he would? He should've found her by now and seen with his own eyes that she was okay, and that this separation was still what she wanted.

"The newspapers have certainly taken Ruby's side," George said as he flicked through some of the headlines on his screen. "'Tycoon's Pregnant Wife Abandoned,' 'Marriage and Fatherhood Too Much for Playboy Mantazis.' And this one really takes the cake: 'Fleming Heiress Duped into Marrying Millionaire Mantazis.'"

"I don't care what the newspapers say about me." Christo swiveled away from the view. "But I won't have them making up stories about Ruby or suggesting that the charity is tarnished as a result of what's happened. That's ludicrous."

Ruby. Was that the first time he'd said her name aloud in the last seven days? He'd thought it a hundred—no—a thousand times, all day, every day. All he'd wanted was the chance to say it to *her*—in their garden, in their house, in his arms. The loss of her was so huge, so bitingly real, that he could almost touch it, and it was growing deeper every day.

"Seems they've interviewed a disgruntled ex-manager from one of your San Francisco resorts," George said. "He says, and I quote, 'Christo Mantazis is a man with an immigrant's chip on his shoulder. He'll push everyone and everything aside to get what he wants, including a brand new wife and baby.'"

Christo knew exactly which worm that would be. The one he'd fired then sued for the sexual harassment of one of his best personal trainers.

"What would you like me to do?" George sat back in his chair.

Ignoring the question, Christo leaned across his desk

and called through the open door. “Patrice, get me Lorenzo Cacciatore on the line.” He pulled in a sharp breath. “I need to find Ruby. Make sure she’s protected from those parasites. Her uncle will know where she is.” The thought of her dealing with all of this alone caused anger to fill the part of his soul that had felt empty all week.

A moment later his phone buzzed, and he picked it up.

“Christo.” Lorenzo’s strong accent came down the line.

Christo leaned his elbows on the desk, a fist clenched in an open palm. “Lorenzo, tell me where Ruby is.”

The older man cleared his throat. “Ah, Christo, I’ve wanted to call and offer my condolences for what has happened with you and Ruby, but Sophia asked me not to. I wish I could help you both.”

“Thank you for the thought, Lorenzo. I need an address where I can find her.”

Lorenzo’s voice grew more desperate. “I wondered about telling you, but Ruby said she needed some time alone and that she didn’t want anyone, especially you, knowing where she is.”

“I’ve stayed away at her wishes, but things have changed.” Christo squeezed his fist as he watched George pull up more articles. “This story has become huge, and she may be dealing with the media fallout on her own. I need to find her before they do.” The thump in his head got stronger.

There was a pause, and then Ruby’s uncle spoke again. “It’s too late for that, Christo. The media have already found her.”

Christo powered to his feet, blood pumping at his temples. “What do you mean?”

“She was on the midday television news half an hour

ago." The older man's voice wavered. "She gave an interview."

Five minutes later, Christo had Googled the television news story and waited while the video footage rolled out. He'd sent George to find the person who'd filed the story, but in the meantime he wanted to see the evidence for himself. He gripped the chair's armrests until his knuckles throbbed. She shouldn't have to deal with this by herself. He should be there to protect her. The empty feeling grew wider and he flicked the mouse on his desk, impatient for news of her.

The newsreader's face filled the screen of the computer, but as the story was being introduced, Christo's gaze was drawn to the image behind him.

A wedding snap of Ruby filled the rest of the screen, and all air was sucked from his lungs. He hadn't had time to look at the prints the photographer had sent through last week, but someone had gotten hold of them. And this one was incredible. Ruby's honey-blonde hair was draped over her shoulders, the delicate veil she wore misting her face. He was surprised at the way he stood, his arm dragging her closer as he looked into her eyes. Her perfect face was lit with a smile. Now the hole in his chest widened, pouring a deep, pervading ache through his whole body, and he steadied himself against the desk.

"...And earlier today, our reporter, Rose Coppen, was at the scene and filed this report."

Christo was glued to the screen, and when he saw Ruby emerge from the front of a tiny house, his heart rate spiked. He curled a fist as he whispered her name. The house looked grimy and run-down, and the noise of traffic in the distance indicated it was in the middle of town.

She stood on a top step, a light cotton dress fitting across her slight shoulders and hugging the perfectly curved shape of her belly. He swallowed.

Hard.

God, he'd missed her. The clean, lavender scent of her shampoo when he buried his face in her hair, the sight of her making jewelry at the kitchen table, the feel of her ripening body as he wrapped his arms around her... His mind flashed to her in his bed, to the sound of her sighs as she snuggled into him after they'd made love, and to their bodies fitting together like two puzzle pieces. But she didn't want a life with him in that house.

A dull throb began at the base of his skull, and he pushed his fingers against his eyes. She wanted more than he could give, and it killed him.

"Mrs. Mantazis," a voice called, and he focused back on the screen. "As he's done right throughout his career, Christo Mantazis has refused to answer any questions about his personal life. Is it true that he left you homeless and pregnant after only weeks of marriage?"

Flashes went off as a scrum of photographers moved forward, and Ruby's eyes rounded as her lips parted. Christo moved closer to the screen, cursing those strangers for wanting something from her that she shouldn't have to give.

"There's a reason why Mr. Mantazis doesn't want to discuss the breakdown of our marriage." She paused, and for a heart-stopping second Christo willed himself through the screen to protect her and that precious baby she was carrying from this outrage. What he wouldn't give for the chance to take her in his arms and take her away from all that.

"The reason he doesn't want to speak about it is that it was my decision. I asked Christo for a divorce."

Chatter broke out and more questions began firing from

every direction. "Was that because he'd misrepresented himself to you?" someone shouted. "That he wanted access to your family estate? Was Mr. Mantazis untrustworthy, Mrs. Mantazis?"

Ruby clasped her hands in front of her and turned her face to the camera. "My name is Ruby Fleming." Her voice was rock solid and it caused pride to burn through him. "And there's not a man in this state who's more generous, more caring, or more trustworthy than Christo Mantazis. He's offered my baby and me a home. He's followed through on every promise he's made since I've been back in Brentwood Bay. He didn't speak to the media about our marriage breakdown because I asked him not to."

She really thought those things about him? After everything that had happened, she was prepared to stand up and put the record straight?

Christo's chest hollowed and words Ruby spoke a long time ago came racing into his head. '*Faith is earned through identifiable actions*,' she'd said. And in her actions right now, in standing up for him when he most needed her, she was showing her faith in him. She could have used this as an opportunity to say that their marriage had been all an act, that she'd gone through with it to get what she wanted—just as she'd thrown at him years before—but she hadn't. Confusion roiled through his whole body, and it felt as though a whole new Ruby had reached in and kissed his heart. A new sensation began to fizz within him, filling his limbs, his chest, and his throat. It made him want to stay and fight for *her*. *Show* he had faith in her and so much more.

"Is there any possibility of a reconciliation, Mrs. Mantazis?" another reporter asked, and Christo drew closer to the screen, every muscle tightening in his body as he drew a deep breath. Her face was in extreme close-up. The blue of her eyes dulled, but the resolution in her voice was crisp and definite. “No, there isn’t. Christo and I want very different things in life. We always have. Christo’s found what he wants, but I’m still looking. I offer him my best.”

Blood roared in his ears, and he had to force himself to continue listening.

“What’ll you do now, Mrs. Mantazis?” another reporter asked.

“I’m going back to New York to resume my publishing career.”

Christo clicked off the screen and stood, fingers curling around the desk as a realization came to him. Ruby wouldn’t be leaving Brentwood Bay. She wouldn’t have to give up the house that she’d grown to love. It was the thing that Ruby wanted most in the world for herself and her baby.

And he was going to give it to her.

12

As dusk painted the summer sky a rich tangerine, Christo pulled his car up to the house he'd seen on a screen earlier in the day and got out. He'd had one of his contacts at the TV station provide the address, and it was as undesirable as he'd expected.

He'd wanted to get to Ruby sooner, but he'd had to speak to his mother, visit a number of people, including his lawyer, and have papers drawn up. It had all taken time, and his head was thumping. When he saw Ruby, he'd put this whole forsaken mess right. Maybe then the cavernous hole in his chest that had grown wider in the last few days would subside.

He would do, *could* do the right thing. Ruby had taught him that. If she believed actions spoke of faith, and trust, and love, then he couldn't wait to show her what he'd started.

The media had dispersed save for a lone paparazzo who was already snapping pictures of him from the opposite curb. He'd considered summoning Ruby to a secret location so that none of this could be scrutinized, but then he'd decided, why bother? Few members of the public would still be interested in his marriage break-up thanks to the way Ruby had set the story straight today.

A vision of her on the TV news raced through his mind, and the same feeling he'd had when she'd stood up for him in front of all those people touched him now. Humbled, proud, and... He took a deeper breath. Another feeling sent deep and aching need pounding through his body each time he thought of her.

Love.

He loved Ruby for her selflessness, for the way she fought for what was right, the way she walked her talk about actions counting more than words. He loved Ruby Fleming for making him look deep within himself and for giving him the courage to trust again.

Suddenly, the resolve he'd felt only hours ago when he'd put alternate plans into place wavered. He had to give Ruby a choice, show her he trusted her judgment when it really counted. That he'd wager his future on her wishes alone.

What if she chose the plan that would drive a stake straight through his heart? He rubbed at his throbbing temple and put every ounce of faith he had into believing Ruby would make the right decision. If she was capable of standing up for him, he was ready to fight for her.

He flicked off a piece of paint peeling from the door and knocked. He'd told her via text that he was coming, and the only reply he'd had was *You'll need to come today, my flight home is booked for tomorrow*. It was good to think she wouldn't be staying in this dive much longer. He shoved a hand inside his trouser pocket. No matter which option Ruby chose, she'd be back where she belonged—in the house where her face lit up, where her laugh could fly free. Where she could let go of the shackles of the past.

As the door pulled open and Ruby looked up at him with luminous blue eyes, his heart beat out of his chest. He gripped the rough wood of the doorjamb and prayed he could see this through. Her eyes were soft, her face make-up free, her smile glowing and open. A hit of something he hadn't felt in a decade tore through his veins like a long craved drug. Right at this moment he wanted this woman with every fiber of his being. He wanted to hold her, love her, and be everything she wanted.

But he'd had this feeling for Ruby once before, and he'd run from it when he'd been exposed and vulnerable. This time he'd face it head on.

Ruby and her unborn child didn't need him to be weak. They needed him to be strong and decisive. When Ruby chose one of his two plans, she could live the life she deserved with her child. The sooner he did this, the sooner this agonizing pain that was gnawing at him would ease.

"Come in." She waved a delicate hand. Her voice was more fragile than he'd heard it before, and he worried about what all this stress had done to her and the precious baby she was carrying. "I hope you don't mind, but I'm packing and I need to keep going if I'm to get everything ready for tomorrow." Her hair was caught up at the back of her head, her silky neck exposed with tantalizing wisps of blonde hair spilling out at will. A tiny black smudge dusted her perfect cheek, and he burned to drag his thumb across it, then reach down and claim her mouth one more time. But this wasn't about what he desired anymore. This was about giving Ruby the chance to live the way she truly wanted.

He stepped into a long hallway, and, as she turned to lead him down it, he noticed the swell of her belly. The way her body was rounding made him pull in a breath. An image of the baby on the ultrasound screen whispered through his mind, but he pushed it aside. He had to. The pain was too big to swallow. The thought that he was so close to losing not just Ruby but also this child was too much to think about. "Leave that a moment," he said as she moved toward an open suitcase in a dimly lit living room. "What I've come with will change your plans."

She clasped her small hands in front of her and blew out a breath, the sound like an arrow to his resolve. "I know what you've come here to say, Christo." Determination laced her voice as she shook her head slowly, and another perfect blonde ringlet escaped. "You've come to try and change the choices I've made. You'll try to convince me that we can make the marriage work, but you're wrong." She sat on the edge of an armchair and hugged her body.

"I haven't come to persuade you to stay with me. I've come to give you a choice for your future." He forced calm into his voice and took the chair opposite. "And whichever option you choose, you'll have your home back."

Her lips parted. "What?"

"I've talked to my mother and we've both signed the house over to you. You can stay. It'll be solely yours as you've always wanted."

There was silence for a moment before Ruby's voice wavered. "But wasn't this all about your mother *having* to stay in the house? Wasn't this all about you acquiring *her* home? We went through with the marriage, living in the house together because there *was* no other way. What's changed now?"

Instead of the pain in his chest easing, it was burning sharper, cutting deeper. *I've changed*, he wanted to say. *I've seen the Ruby I came so close to loving in the past, and I can't turn my back on you this time. But I have to be sure the choice is yours*. He pulled his spine straighter. No matter what she decided, what he was about to say would give Ruby a chance at the life she really wanted. That was all that mattered.

"I've always said that my mother would only be happy back in Greece or in your home. But in the last week I've realized that she felt so at home in your parents' house because of the people in it. At first it was your family, then just Antonia. Most recently you. Now Mom wants to be where I am, and I've told her that depends on you."

Ruby's face paled as she laid a steadying hand on the back of the chair and stood. "Why me?"

His throat burned as the words bled out. "I want you to make the decision about where I'll live. And there are two options."

Ruby shook her head in confusion while Christo kept speaking. "The first option involves the fact that I've bought the house next door. It's somewhere Mom knows well and she'll still have her neighborhood friends. But most importantly it will mean she and I can still be in your baby's life. We'd be there when you need us, we'd be a part of each other's lives as we'd planned, but it would give you the space for your own life and your own relationships. That's choice number one."

Ruby put a hand across her mouth to smother her shock and her grinding disappointment. When Christo had sent the text to say he was coming she'd had the crazy, unwarranted hope that he'd come to persuade her to return to their marriage, and she hadn't been sure she wouldn't bend to his wishes.

That treacherous voice in her head had said he'd missed her, that he'd wanted to be with her as something so much more than a convenient wife. Deep in her heart she'd let herself hope that Christo had finally realized he *could* love her and her baby. She'd hoped that instead of removing himself from her as he'd always done, this time he'd stand beside her, ready to face the world together.

But he hadn't come to do that at all. Despite the look of soft strength in him, he'd come to ask her to open her heart wider. Have him so near her life and yet so far away. It was too cruel to contemplate, but not as cruel as what she guessed her other choice would be. He'd said there was only one other place his mother would be happy—Greece. He was going to move to the other side of the world, and she'd be left with the house and the memories of him in every corner.

From somewhere deep within her a sob worked its way up through her body, growing in size so that it blocked her throat, stung the back of her nose, and made her lungs desperate for breath. She pushed it away. He'd never offered her anything more than what they'd had. It was her own fault that she'd fallen in love with him.

"Ruby, what is it?" Christo stood, and the memory of being wrapped in his protective hug caused her throat to close tighter.

"I know what my second choice is going to be. It's to have you and your mother move back to Greece, away from me and my baby," she said as tears began to burn. "I know I shouldn't be surprised by that. I've done exactly what I accused you of doing. When the going got tough I turned and ran instead of facing up to love, looking it straight in the eye, and embracing it. And now it's too late. I don't know if I can bear living in that house with the memory of everything we shared there."

"No, it's not too late." He moved toward her. His mouth curved upwards and light shined in his face.

With every ounce of strength she could muster, she steadied her voice and squeezed his arm. "Thank you so much, Christo. That you would give up the house for me means so much." She drew a deeper breath. "I'm sure you'll find happiness in Greece, and I hope with all my heart that you can be a father one day." She leaned closer and placed her lips on his, one final time drinking in his marine scent, the warmth of his skin, and the certainty that surrounded everything he did.

As her lips began to tremble, she pulled back and looked deep in his eyes. "You'll make an incredible father. You have so much to offer a child and so much to offer a woman that you love."

She looked away, knowing she couldn't hide the tears that were about to fall. Could her mother have imagined this scene when she'd written her will? That Christo would be giving her the house, or that Ruby's heart would be breaking for the second time in her life over the loss of Christo Mantazis?

Christo gripped her hand, and she lifted her misting gaze to his. "I feel like the father of *your* child. And for that reason the second choice is not Greece. I'm not going to turn my back and run from you the way I've done in the past. Ruby, I want to be a part of your baby's life forever."

Her heart stopped, and she searched his face. "What do you mean?" she whispered.

He squeezed her fingers more firmly. "When I saw my lawyer today, I not only signed my share of the house to you, I also changed my will. This baby will be my sole beneficiary." He picked up her other hand. "When I saw that baby on the ultrasound screen, when I realized the love you had for that tiny being, I realized I loved that child, too. Because you're his or her mother. And today I realized that I can't be apart from him or from you. You've moved me, Ruby, to look deep inside and face down my hurt pride of ten years ago, and in doing that I've found the sort of love I never knew existed."

"Oh, Christo." She pulled him close so that his heart beat next to hers, and she buried her face in his neck. "You don't know what that means to me. For so long I've wanted to hear you say you'd love this baby."

Christo lifted her chin and with aching tenderness kissed her lips. It was the sweetest kiss they'd ever shared, full of trust and understanding.

"What's the second choice?" she whispered.

"Your second choice is to give me the chance to be everything you want in a husband and father. I want us to be a family, Ruby. I want to grow with you, learn with you, *be* with you. I want to love you and our baby, but whichever option you choose I want to be near this child forever. I'm done running from love. I've found it in you and I'm here to stay. I love you, Ruby Fleming."

Ruby closed her eyes and let Christo's beautiful, genuine, heartfelt words wash over her, and then she leaned closer and kissed him on the mouth. "You came here today to give me what I wanted most in the world," she said through trembling lips. "And now I have it. I see that you love our baby and me. I *see* that you trust me, that you'll stay around, that you'll face love head-on, and that you want to build a real relationship with me. I love you, Christo. For all you do, for everything you believe in, and for the way you've made me feel, I love you. I'll take the second choice."

"I love you, too." Christo wrapped her in his arms and pulled her into a passionate kiss that took her breath away.

EPILOGUE

Ruby held her phone up and swiped to the camera. For a moment, objects in the small square were a fuzzy jumble, but she moved a little closer and everything jumped into crisp focus.

A warm glow began inside her as Christo's rugged jaw, darkened from weekend stubble and damp from pool water, filled the frame. Then, as she moved slightly to the right, the image changed, and her heart swelled in her chest.

Now that strong, masculine face was cheek-to cheek with another—the sweetly grinning face of their beautiful son, Niko. For an exquisite moment she was transfixed by the image of father and son in the water as Christo whispered something in the little boy's ear, and they both chuckled.

Touched by the unforgettable beauty of the image, Ruby placed the phone on the table beside her, wanting to seal this vision deep in her memory.

"*Ela, Niko*," her mother-in-law, Stella, said as she moved to the side of the pool, arms draped in a towel. "Come to *Yiayia*. I've made you some *tiropites* for your dinner."

Ruby smiled as her son lifted his arms to his grandmother, and Christo passed him out of the pool.

"Have a swim, Ruby," Stella said as she cuddled the little boy tight in the towel. "You must be exhausted after everything you've done with Niko today. I'll tell Diana to serve dinner when he is asleep."

"Thank you, Stella." Ruby blew a kiss to her little boy. "Bye-bye, sweetheart. Enjoy your cheese pies. I'll come and tuck you in."

Niko planted a kiss in the middle of his chubby palm and threw the kiss back to her. Then he took his grandmother's hand, and they walked toward the terrace.

Ruby padded barefoot to the side of the pool, basking in the warmth of her husband's gaze on her bikini-clad body. Christo moved slowly through the water until he reached her at the pool steps. He tilted his chin, and a sexy smile painted his face. "Have I told you how beautiful you look?"

She smiled at the words he'd used every day of their new life, and as had happened each time he'd said them, her body ached to be close to him.

She took the hand he held out to her, and when he squeezed her fingers, a feeling of completeness swept over her. Moving down the pool steps, goosebumps raced across her skin but were banished as Christo drew her close, his strong arms enveloping her. "It's been too long," he whispered into her hair.

She placed a kiss at his throat, the tang of chlorine mixing with the warmth of his skin on her lips. "What's been too long?" She leaned back to look into his face.

"Since I could hold you this close and tell you how much I love you."

"We made love this morning, sweetheart," she whispered. "You held me close then. Have you forgotten already?"

"Forgotten?" A smile touched his mouth. "I can remember every single time we've made love in the last two years."

She widened her eyes in pretend surprise. "*Every* time?"

He leaned down and laid a kiss at the corner of her lips. "From our first time, right up until today. Every place, every minute. Every sensation."

"That's a lot to remember," Ruby teased. She kissed him back while his hands caressed the skin at her shoulders. She decided to tease him further. "Can you pick a favorite time?"

Christo lifted his chin, his eyes narrowed in mock concentration. "The *most* memorable?"

Ruby held her breath, the joking suddenly forgotten as she wanted to hear which time he'd felt the closest to her, experienced the greatest feeling of love. She wanted to give him that feeling all over again.

"I think it would have to be the time beside the pool," he said.

Her heart sank a little, but she stroked the firm muscles along his arm. "We've never made love by the pool."

"Of course we have." He pulled her close so her own heart began beating with the rhythm of his. "Don't you remember that evening when I laid you out on the grass and told you I was the happiest man in the world?" He slid a finger under the strap at her shoulder. "The time you wore that sexy black bikini."

"No," she said, and then she saw the glint in his eye grow brighter. "Unless you're talking about the evening when our beautiful son was inside with his grandmother eating cheese pies." She slid her own hand around to the top of his swim shorts. "The time you wore those tropical design shorts I love so much."

"Yes, that was the night," he said. He cupped her face in his hands and looked deep in her eyes. "That night and every night after."

With his kiss warm and firm on her mouth, Ruby melted into his embrace, the beauty of their life together filling her soul.

***

Read the next book in the **Tall, Dark and Driven** series!

A Family for Good is Markus's story.

Read an excerpt from ***A Family for Good*** on the next few pages.

Buy ***A Family for Good*** from your local book store, Amazon, or ask for it at your local library.

REVIEW A MARRIAGE FOR SHOW

If you've really enjoyed *A Marriage for Show,* it would mean the world to me if you could leave me a review.

Great reviews help enormously to bring my books to the attention of other readers like you who may enjoy them.

To leave a review, go to www.amazon.com and search for **A Marriage for Show**.

Thank you!!

GET A FREE NOVELLA

Throughout my career, my readers have been such a key part of my writing life and I love to keep them up to date with what I'm doing. I occasionally send out newsletters with details on new releases and extra special offers for both my books and those like mine. I promise I won't bombard you!

If you sign up to the mailing list, the first thing I'll send you is a **FREE** novella, ***Waiting on Forever***, the prequel to my ***Tall, Dark and Driven*** series.

Waiting on Forever

One last task to complete, then Alex Panos can fulfill a heart breaking promise. That is, if he can get past cute and quirky Mara Hemmingway.

On her own since she was sixteen, Mara won't be taken advantage of again—especially not by brooding and troubled Alex. Instead, she'll play him at his own game.

When their powerful attraction threatens to get in the way of both their dreams, someone will have to face a future of waiting on forever.

You can get the novella by emailing
barb@barbaradeleo.com!

NEXT IN THE TALL, DARK AND DRIVEN SERIES

A FAMILY FOR GOOD - MARKUS'S STORY

She won't let her heart be broken again. He'll do whatever it takes to protect twin baby girls. On the island of Aphrodite, they'll both have to trust if they're to receive the greatest gift of all.

Perfumer Liv Bailey's in Cyprus to claim custody of twin baby girls after her best friend died alone giving birth. The one thing standing between Liv and a fresh start in Brentwood Bay with the babies, is Markus Nicoliedies, the man Liv was forced to leave five years ago.

Markus has given up on love. When Liv left him in Paris on the day of his grandfather's funeral, he vowed never to open himself up again. But when an old friend asked if she could name him as her twins' father, rather than leave them vulnerable to her violent partner, he couldn't say no.

Forced to live together while waiting for a custody decision, both Liv and Markus have to fight the powerful attraction that still exists between them.

You can read an extract from **A Family for Good** on the next page.

Buy ***A Family for Good*** from your local book store, Amazon, or ask for it at your local library.

A FAMILY FOR GOOD

Nicosia, Cyprus

Five minutes.

If she could make it through the next five minutes without shattering into tiny little pieces and skidding across this shiny marble floor, Liv Bailey could face another day.

She could do five minutes. She'd done it to have blood drawn, or a tooth extracted...

In the next five minutes she'd confront the man she'd once loved. She'd sit down with Markus Panos, discuss the future of the precious newborn twins in his care, and tell him she intended to take them away with her.

Then she'd leave him behind, as fast as she possibly could.

She'd done that before—left, that is—and though she'd done it five years ago to keep her sanity and life intact, the pain of having to leave her heart behind back then stabbed like needles behind her travel weary eyes.

But things were different now.

Now thoughts of the past came second to babies she knew she'd love as her own.

She was desperate to see them.

They *had* to make this work. She and Markus owed it to her best friend Polly, and to the baby girls left motherless when Polly had died so unexpectedly.

Markus could never be anything other than an Indiana Jones in a two-thousand-dollar suit, while she valued the quiet life...no risks, no injuries, *no heartache.*

Polly wouldn't rest in peace if she knew her best friend had left the babies with someone who lived life on the edge. They'd known each other since meeting in a foster home at age nine. They'd been like sisters.

"He shouldn't be much longer," the woman behind the desk said in a heavy Greek accent, and Liv nodded, absently looking around the walls while her stomach churned.

What *was* this place? With everything written in Greek, she couldn't guess what kind of business he was in. She'd expected the taxi from the airport to take her to an inner city law firm, not a huge building on the outskirts of Nicosia, the island's largest city.

They could be in any reception area anywhere in the world, except the fittings in this one—the marble floor, the chestnut leather couches—indicated that whatever happened in this company, it was very successful.

"You have a hotel?"

Heat arced through her as she spun around. And just like that, Markus was standing there making polite conversation, and the last five years tumbled back in on themselves as she looked into the depths of his rich brown eyes.

She swallowed and stood on liquid legs, willing away the burn of longing she'd known would flame as soon as she saw him, her heart bruising her chest wall as it hammered ever faster.

Not a muscle on his perfect tan face moved; not a blink, not a hint of emotion or remembrance crossed his sculpted jaw. He stood like one of the ancient statues housed in museums only a few miles away from here - taut and male and with a history she knew as well as her own.

To cover the tremble in her voice, she employed her best business tone and smoothed down her skirt. "Markus. You *are* here." Not quite the practiced and confident words of reunion she'd dreamed of.

Five minutes.

"I didn't expect you 'til tomorrow," he said as he flicked through papers on the reception desk. "As I'm unavailable for the rest of the afternoon, my PA will arrange a more appropriate time for a meeting."

Clutching the folder in her hand tighter, she tried to right the tilt everything had suddenly acquired. "We need to talk about Phoebe and Zoë now," she said, and threw a quick look as the secretary drew in a noisy breath. "We need to make plans. I'm grateful for what you've done, but Polly would've wanted *me* to be the guardian of the girls. I need to take them back with me. I need to take them home."

Her shoulders slumped.

There. She'd said it in one big rush. It was out in the open and she held her breath waiting for his response.

Something crossed his face, a softening at the name of her best friend who'd died so suddenly, and Liv could see the composed businessman replaced by the protective partner who'd once melted her time and again.

"There won't be any fighting."

His words coiled tight around her, the accent emphasizing the strength and defense in his voice.

She'd heard that tone five years ago. When she'd had to save herself before she fell apart...

Markus Panos took too many risks, the sort of risks that cost Liv's biological parents their lives. If you loved someone, if they depended on you, you safeguarded your life. It was as simple as that.

"I see you've come prepared." He looked down at the custody and emigration papers she clutched in her hand.

"We have an appointment with Child and Family Services tomorrow to discuss custody and the girls' long-term care. Can you make it?"

"Of course."

Did he honestly feel no connection to her? He didn't remember what they'd shared? Or had he been too affected by what she'd had to do in the past? He spoke in Greek to the secretary who pursed her magenta lips before stalking past them to an inner office.

Liv sighed and shook her head. "I can't imagine how hard it must've been on you."

"I've done what was necessary. What Polly asked me to do in her final hours." His tone was dismissive.

"I'm sure it's been a struggle you'll be glad to be relieved of." Her voice quavered at the thought of everything that had happened in the last few weeks, but she forced herself to say it all. "Polly dying, the funeral, wondering how to take care of the girls... I don't know how you've managed to cope, but I'm ready to take over."

Still he looked down and then slowly lifted his gaze to her, and for the first time she noticed the pinched skin around his tired eyes.

"You know it's the best thing for everyone, don't you? Phoebe and Zoë..." Her throat ached over the words. "They need a mother."

"What they need is security. *Consistency*."

Liv bit her lip. She was so thankful he'd rescued the girls when Polly had no one else in Cyprus to turn to. Liv had done everything she could to track Polly down, but she'd drawn a blank until Markus had called her with the devastating news.

She spoke more softly. "You shouldn't be expected to look after newborn twins."

His gaze remained hooked on the marble floor while a muscle in his jaw flexed twice.

"Where are Phoebe and Zoë now?"

His strong, chiseled face darkened before the thick-lashed black eyes leveled on her and flashed. "I haven't neglected them, if that's what you're suggesting."

"But are they *your* babies? I'm assuming they aren't if you didn't stop me coming here."

A shudder dropped through her centre. The question had slipped out before she could catch it. They hadn't discussed the matter of paternity on the phone. She'd assumed when he hadn't told her to mind her own business and stay away that he mustn't be their father.

"The babies are my responsibility."

It wasn't a real answer, but she had to go on believing he wasn't their dad. If she didn't push doubts and questions away now she wouldn't have the strength to see this through.

He leaned a little closer as if to make a connection. His lips tightened and the air between them sparked before he dropped his head and looked away.

"You've come from Geneva?" He spoke quietly, ignoring the paternity question hanging in the air.

"Yes, I've been living there, but I'll be returning to the Brentwood Bay now, of course."

"I trust you've found a hotel for the next few days?"

"Yes, thank you," she said with ridiculous formality. She placed her bag on the counter-top to underline the fact she'd stay here until she got what she'd come to secure. "But I imagine I'll be here longer than a few days. Custody and emigration could take a while."

He stayed silent, the angle of his head indicating he was sizing up her response and not necessarily agreeing with it.

She tried a smile. "The hotel's in the middle of Nicosia, by a lovely old stone wall."

He nodded. "You have everything you need?"

"For now."

He was standing an inch too close...and he was too intensely masculine, too rigidly beautiful. He was everything she'd ever wanted in a man, and everything she could never have.

Loving Markus Panos had almost destroyed her once. *Never again.*

Frustrated, she turned away from the intensity of his stare, noticing something strange, something she'd sensed while she sat waiting. She lifted her chin and inhaled.

Lemon.

The whole place smelled of lemon. Not the antiseptic aroma of a citrus floor cleaner or the sickly synthetic scent of artificial air freshener. This smelled like *real* lemon, the sharp tang of a pitcher of homemade lemonade, or the bite of a cool lemon mousse. Very strange for an office environment—but beautiful.

Holding his proud stare—the one that used to make her feel special, cherished—she cleared her throat and balled her hands into private fists, fighting the overwhelming desire to get mad at this intensely uncomfortable situation. She wanted something, two things, very badly, and he was the only one who could give them to her.

"Do you live close?"

Be polite, stay calm.

His words were flat. "There's no need to talk about me." With a self-controlled click, he'd locked the door she'd closed on him five years ago.

She raised her eyes to the ceiling and counted to three. "Markus, I know you've said you were the only person Polly knew in Cyprus, but she would've wanted *me* to have custody of the girls if anything happened to her. She had no relatives and we were best friends. We shared all the highs and lows in our lives and we trusted each other. So either we talk now, or it'll have to be done through lawyers."

He blinked slowly, the way she remembered, and her heart skipped a beat as he leaned closer. And then another five-word sentence. "I'll give you fifteen minutes."

He turned then and walked down a marbled corridor, and Liv scolded herself for not handling this better. She wished she could just *talk* to him, without feeling she had to prove why she should have custody of the girls.

Striding behind him, she took quick glances at the huge Grecian artworks hanging on the walls as sharp light shone down from an atrium ceiling.

When they reached the lift, he swiped a card and stood still, staring straight ahead. She couldn't, wouldn't, allow her hungry eyes a glance as she stood rigid, but she could sense him, smell him—a fragrance of newly hewn wood and cinnamon. The scent of Markus.

He was everything she remembered—mysterious, but with a zest for life that seemed to radiate from every part of him.

A jolt of unbidden awareness ran through her.

She concentrated on the lift too, her heart hollow. He'd always been so animated, intense...not silent and angry. He'd been a lot like Polly really.

Polly...

Tears crept up again, but she pushed them swiftly away. Now was the time to be strong.

His office was on the top floor, and Markus held the door open as she walked in.

The panorama beyond almost took her breath away. Across high rise buildings and ancient churches, everything terracotta and beige—the color of the desert—her gaze stretched out to the stark hills beyond. Palm trees dotted boulevards, and everything shimmered as the Middle Eastern sun tracked to its high point in the sky.

The smell of lemon was gone, but it was replaced by the rich, buttery scent of nuts. Hazelnuts. Her brow creased as she looked around for the source, but nothing was obvious.

"I'm sorry for your loss." Markus indicated a chair, and Liv sat, although he stayed standing.

"And yours."

So formal. Her heart dropped. No one witnessing this would've believed them lovers five years ago.

As she settled into the cushioning comfort of the leather seat her heartbeat kicked up a gear. The strain of seeing him again was replaced by a desperate need to make a connection with him now. Time for honesty.

"What happened between you and Polly, Markus?" The words rushed out with less subtlety than she'd hoped, and heat lit her cheeks. "The hospital says she wasn't clear about who the father is and I don't want...I can't understand..."

His throat moved in an awkward swallow and he looked down briefly before tilting his head and fixing his gaze directly on her. "Polly was new to Cyprus and in trouble as she told you, I believe. She'd been running from some things in her past and contacted me to help when she became ill very shortly after the girls' birth. I don't think either of us..." He stopped, and Liv watched his Adam's apple move up and down in tight jumps.

The honest nature of his words, his real emotion and attempt to explain were not what she'd expected and her chest pulled tight. She *so* wanted to believe he wasn't their father...that he and Polly hadn't...

He clearly didn't want to go further and what right did she have now to ask him something so intimate?

But she had to know. If he was Phoebe and Zoë's father, then no matter how strongly she felt about him having custody she had no legal rights here. "I have to know. It changes—"

"Of course you do, and you will. But not right now. After we've met with Child and Family Services you'll know everything. But not before."

He'd cut across her words with such pace and passion that her mouth remained open as he hurried on. "Phoebe and Zoë are fine. They're being taken care of as they should be." And although she wanted to press him further, she was pulled up by the way his voice and face softened when he talked about the girls; her heart sped at the way their names fell effortlessly from his mouth.

"Who by?"

"They're with a nanny while I'm at work, until I can arrange something more satisfactory."

Uncomfortable at being on this side of a desk—at a decided disadvantage—Liv pulled herself higher in her chair. "When Polly found out she was pregnant, she asked me to be godmother. So, unless..." Unless he *was* the girls' father.

He did the slow blink thing again and crossed muscular arms across his taut chest, wordless. Her heart thundered, mouth dry with the thought that he was closed to her.

She pushed on. "She couldn't possibly have imagined things would turn out like this..."

"She told you she had escalated blood pressure? That they were worried about her even before the birth?"

A curl of nausea crept its way from her stomach to her throat. No words would come.

"She *told* you her life was in danger?"

Her throat tightened and the smell of nuts became stronger, sickening. All Liv knew was that Polly had gone into early labor and was making her way to the hospital and then she stopped replying to Liv's texts. Liv had called all the people they knew in common, rung welfare agencies and the American consulate in Cyprus but hadn't found a trace of her. What if she'd tried harder, gotten on a plane sooner and kept hunting until she'd found Polly? How might things be different?

"Could I have a glass of water?" she finally managed to wring out.

He pushed a button at his desk and spoke quickly to someone, the metallic cut of his foreign words making her feel no better. He'd never spoken Greek when they'd lived together in Paris. There hadn't been a need.

They'd been lovers. So deeply committed to each other. She'd believed they'd always be together. The reality that he was such a stranger now dug painfully deep.

"You knew she was having problems?" His tone was more gentle.

Her voice quavered as she replied to the first personal words he'd given her; it brought him, the old Markus, so close she could almost feel him. "Yes, she said her boyfriend had hit her once or twice, but when I tried to discuss it with her she'd shut down. If only I..."

"This must've been a huge shock, then." He leaned against the side of the desk, his mouth moving into a gentle smile. The door opened and a young woman brought in a silver tray with two bottles of mineral water and two squat crystal tumblers. She placed them on the desk and left.

He continued quietly. "She'd said she'd been in touch with you, but she became very sick during labor. I promised that if anything happened I'd arrange for Phoebe and Zoë to have the best possible care, that I'd contact you at the first opportunity...which I did."

He unscrewed a bottle and poured the water into a glass before passing it to her. Her hand looked pale and small against his and, for a moment, she remembered how secure she felt when he used to hold it. "It was difficult to track you down," he said.

She heard the insinuation in his voice. The question about how stable, how reliable she'd be in the future forced her to reply. "You know the fragrance world," she said, hating that she had to explain. "I travel a lot and was in Paris when you called me. But that'll all change when I take Phoebe and Zoë back to Brentwood Bay. My foster parents want to help me take care of the girls, and when I'm ready I can take on new development work in the U.S arm of the business."

He walked over to the window and stood with his back to her. She noticed the fingers of one hand drum his elbow. He'd done that in the past, when he'd thought deeply about something.

No, she would *not* remember.

He spoke again, his voice cool, controlled. "This is a difficult situation. I'm custodian of two vulnerable children whose existence I didn't know of three weeks ago. I must be certain—"

"The *custodian*..." His choice of word caused her throat to catch.

His face read irritation, but his voice remained steady. "As Polly asked, they're in my care and arrangements—"

Her throat closed tighter. "*Arrangements*..."

Markus frowned. "I'm talking about the babies' lives and you're pushing me on word choice?"

He had a point. "Look..." She pushed back her chair and stood. "I know you've stepped in to a terrible situation and I'm so grateful for it. But you've done everything you need to and now I'm here to take over. The babies are fragile and...motherless, Markus."

She sucked in her top lip, grateful he was still turned away so he couldn't see it wobble. The grief she'd kept bottled in the last three weeks as she'd tried to establish where Polly was had now inched its way forward.

"I'm sorry." She swayed, her legs barely able to hold her. "This is a very emotional time and I want..." Her words were a tight whisper. "I just want what Polly would've wanted."

He lifted his square jaw higher so the shadow on it appeared a shade darker. "You must see the position I'm in. These babies are precious. You come here saying you're the best person to take care of Phoebe and Zoë, but your actions in the past—the way you run when the going gets tough, the way you move on a whim—suggests that's not true."

The raw honesty of his words thudded in her ears, and she took a step back as if she'd been struck.

"Are you talking about what happened between you and me?" she asked in a strangled whisper.

"Of course I am, Olivia. You walked out on our relationship without any warning, and aside from that you've never lived in one place any real length of time. I won't allow that sort of random behavior around the girls."

It was the first time he'd said her name, and the way his voice caressed and smoothed the word as he'd done so many times softened her response to his suggestion. "I'm here for Phoebe and Zoë now, aren't I?"

He shrugged. "Anyone can turn up for a day."

She swallowed, realizing she might be alienating him with her words. But she knew deep in her heart that they had to work together, acknowledge the power of their past, their intimate knowledge of each other, and then bulldoze those great boulders out of their way.

It was time to change focus. "I really want to see them, Markus." She couldn't cover the crack in her voice.

He rubbed a hand across his jaw, and Liv let out a slow breath. "I know you're protecting them, and that's what I knew you'd do. We've got a lot to go through before all the paperwork's done, but I have to see them. See the last two things Polly touched." The tears fought their way to the surface and she struggled to keep them at bay. "This is unexpected for me as well." Her voice tripped as a tear began its path down her cheek. "At least let me see them. Please."

He began to speak. "It's not—" Then his eyes met hers and the look on his face changed.

Could he still care, at least enough to be moved by her sadness? Liv dragged the inside of her wrist across her cheek. Despite wanting to give in to the weight of her grief she *had* to stay in control. For Phoebe and Zoë.

"Of course." He spoke quietly as he looked at his watch. "At five o'clock this afternoon. They fed at seven this morning, so if their routine's on track that should work." He moved briskly across the room to the door, clearly expecting her to leave.

"Where? Where should I meet you?" Anticipation fluttered in her stomach.

"There's a square, right in front of the Byzantine Museum. We'll be there at five o'clock."

"I could come to your home," she said suddenly. "So the girls aren't unsettled."

His features moved again, the curtain of defense closing once more. "The square is fine. I must protect Phoebe and Zoë in the meantime, Olivia, from anything that might compromise their stability. For now, they're with me, and until I can have an indication that you have their best interests at heart, that you're not going to run when everything gets too difficult..." He towered over her, his jaw tightening. "That's the way it'll remain."

Despite being late afternoon, the majestic Cypriot sun sent a blanket of heat across the ancient square. In the distance, people sat around tables, talking and drinking long coffees, and a priest, like a blackbird on the wing, made his way up the steps of a church.

Although she'd traveled all over the world for business, it was very rare for Liv to be somewhere foreign on her own. Normally she'd have drivers, personal assistants to take care of things for her, but she'd chosen to take this on alone. Alone with the man she'd once loved, with her sense of inadequacy at the possibility of being a parent...

But she'd steeled herself and she was here.

Phoebe and Zoë were all that mattered in the world and she was desperate to see them.

The smell of barbecued food teased her senses, and her stomach growled. She hadn't eaten since breakfast. In fact she'd eaten very little in the last few days since learning of her best friend's death.

Markus had called her three nights ago. He'd been polite, detached on the phone at first, but gentle when he gave her the heartbreaking news. Much of what he'd said had been lost between Liv's sobs, but she'd gained enough understanding to know she had to get to the girls as quickly as she could.

She swiftly scanned the square, wringing her hands at the thought of seeing Markus again. A sense of awareness flushed her cheeks as she turned slowly. Then her heart hit her throat.

There he was. There *they* were. Markus and the girls, turned slightly away from her at the edge of the square.

For some reason she'd expected a nanny or his mother would be with him, taking responsibility for the tiny babies. That he'd have very little to do with their day-to-day care.

But, dressed in a sleek black suit, and looking more protective, more natural than she could ever have imagined, was Markus alone, carefully rocking a double pram backwards and forwards.

Phoebe and Zoë. The only parts left of Polly were just a few feet from Liv now, and she instinctively moved forward, her breath jamming her already clogged chest.

One of the babies let out a cry. Markus bent down, carefully removed the sunshade, and now lifted a tiny bundle into his arms.

And the power of it, the way it caused love and wonder and longing to sweep the length of her body and grip tight around her heart made Liv falter.

She'd assumed he'd be the same—hurried and hyper. That he'd want her to take the babies off his hands as quickly as possible so he could get on with taking risks and putting himself first.

But something about the way he held that precious gift of a girl in the crook of his arm, his head bent toward her face, lips moving in a whisper, made something unravel in Liv's chest. In her wildest dreams she'd never have believed Markus Panos could be so giving, so responsible.

Slowly she made her way toward them, and as she got nearer couldn't speak, the muscles of her throat too crushed by the beauty of what she saw: father and...daughter?

As he returned the quietened baby to the pram, she edged closer and could now see Phoebe and Zoë as two perfect bundles. Their identical heads as round and smooth as river stone, peeked above dusky pink blankets, tiny hands held in the same position by their rosebud mouths.

Fresh tears filled her eyes as she knelt and held out a hand to touch. The warmth of two little bodies seeped into her soul, their breath like a forgotten whisper reaching her straining ears.

She sensed Markus step away.

The sadness of the whole situation scrambled her thoughts. Why had Polly been so secretive about her pregnancy? Why had she never mentioned even meeting up with Markus? And why, oh why, hadn't Liv found her friend in time?

Despite witnessing Markus's care with the girls just now, he'd said he saw himself as *custodian* to these precious babies. Someone who would do the bare minimum to ensure a good outcome for them. But treating their happiness as a problem to be solved or a challenge to tackle wasn't enough. They needed a mother.

Not being a relative to Polly meant Liv's legal rights were zero, and although her experience with children was nil, she knew to her deepest heart that she *would* love these children as madly and deeply as if they were her own.

"They're gorgeous," she whispered, hoping she could make a deeper connection with Markus, lay the groundwork for the discussion that had to be continued. "I never imagined they'd be so tiny."

He stood by, silently watching, and Liv stood to create some link between them, between him and her need to reach out, to smile, to connect.... "I'm sorry you've had to become involved with this. If I'd... If things had worked out differently I could've been here and..."

"But you weren't here, were you?" He spoke so quietly she barely caught his words. "For whatever reason you didn't try hard enough when someone needed you."

Sorrow crashed over her. "I couldn't find her. I didn't even know which country she was in. But none of that matters now. What's important is that I'm here to take the girls back to Brentwood Bay as Polly would've wanted."

He was right. She should've done more, and the pain of knowing she'd let Polly down seared deep.

He removed his glasses, in the slow, deliberate way that reminded her how strong and confident he was.

"We'll work this out, Olivia. For the sake of Phoebe and Zoë we'll find the best possible future for them, but for their stability in the meantime they're staying with me."

He spoke as if she were a stranger, not as a man who'd once held her and said he'd rather stop living than be without her. Her heart spasmed as she forced herself to speak, frustration muscling its way between sorrow for all she'd lost and the measured tone of her words.

She breathed long and deep. "What you're doing, what you've done for Polly and the girls is amazing, Markus, and I know it'll take some time to work things out."

He gripped the handle of the pram before he spoke with quiet conviction, his words wrapping her tight. "I've only done what someone committed to the best for Phoebe and Zoë would do, and I'm wondering if you've really got that sort of commitment too."

Bam.

In one sentence he'd reached the heart of this entire dilemma, past and present together, and she ached. Because she'd left him in the past he didn't think she had the commitment to be there for the girls for the rest of their lives.

She pushed the past aside—she couldn't let it matter now. All that mattered were Phoebe and Zoë, and she wasn't going to leave here without them.

LOVE BARBARA'S BOOKS?

If you really enjoyed *A Marriage for Show* and fancy reading a lot more about the crazy, lovable Katsalos family, as well as Barbara's next series, apply to join Barbara's review team!

Barbara is now taking applications to join her Advanced Review team. If you're selected, you'll get all of Barbara's releases free, up to a month before release!

Email barb@barbaradeleo.com and Barbara will be in touch!

ABOUT BARBARA

Multi award winning author, Barbara DeLeo's first book, co-written with her best friend, was a story about beauty queens in space. She was eleven, and the sole, handwritten copy was lost years ago much to everyone's relief. It's some small miracle that she kept the faith and now lives her dream of writing sparkling contemporary romance with unforgettable characters.

Degrees in English and Psychology, and a career as an English teacher, fueled Barbara's passion for people and stories, and a number of years living in Europe —primarily in Athens, Greece—gave her a love for romantic settings.

Discovering she was having her second set of twins in two years, Barbara knew she must be paying penance for being disorganized in a previous life and now uses every spare second to create her stories.With every word she writes, Barbara is sharing her belief in the transformational power of loving relationships.

Married to her winemaker hero for twenty two years, Barbara's happiest when she's getting to know her latest cast of characters. She still loves telling stories about finding love in all the wrong places, but now without a beauty queen or spaceship in sight.

A Marriage for Show
A Tall, Dark and Driven book
Christo's story
by Barbara DeLeo

Cover Design - Natasha Snow Designs www.natashasnow.com

ALSO BY BARBARA DELEO

The Tall, Dark and Driven series

All books can be read as stand alone

Waiting on Forever—prequel novella ~ **Alex's story** ~ email barb@barbaradeleo.com

Available from your local book store, amazon.com, or ask for it at your local library:

Making the Love List—Book 1~Yasmin's story

Winning the Wedding War—Book 2 ~ Nick's story

Reining in the Rebel —Book 3 ~ Ari's story

A Home for Summer—Book 4 ~ Costa's story

A Family for Good—Book 6 ~ Markus's story

ACKNOWLEDGEMENTS

Not only was I lucky enough to have been born into a wonderfully supportive family where dreams are championed and crazy little quirks celebrated, I've been welcomed into a second family too. Since I met my Greek boyfriend, now husband, thirty years ago, I've been immersed in a culture, a language, and a way of celebrating life that I love. I'd like to thank both families for giving me love, laughter, and inspiration for the story of the Katsalos family in my ***Tall, Dark and Driven*** series.

My heartfelt thanks also goes to:

My agent, Nalini Akolekar, who always has my back and wonderful advice to share.

My incredible crit partners, Hayson Manning and Rachel Bailey, who are amazing writers and save my patootie time and time again.

Iona, Sue, Kate, Courtney, Deborah, Nadine and Naomi who are the BEST group of motivators, cheerleaders and wine drinking pals a girl could have.

My cover designer, Natasha Snow, who nails it every time.

My copy editor Elizabeth King whose Type A attention to detail is legendary.

My proofreader Amy Hart who makes everything shine.

And to George and my four amazing children, thank you for helping me to keep on living this dream. Squeeze, squeeze, squeeze.

Barb **X**